# Frozen Heart

## DEFIANCE

### SKYE MACKINNON

Peryton Press

# FROZEN HEART

USA TODAY BESTSELLING AUTHOR

## SKYE MACKINNON

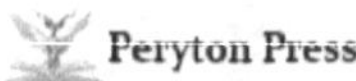 Peryton Press

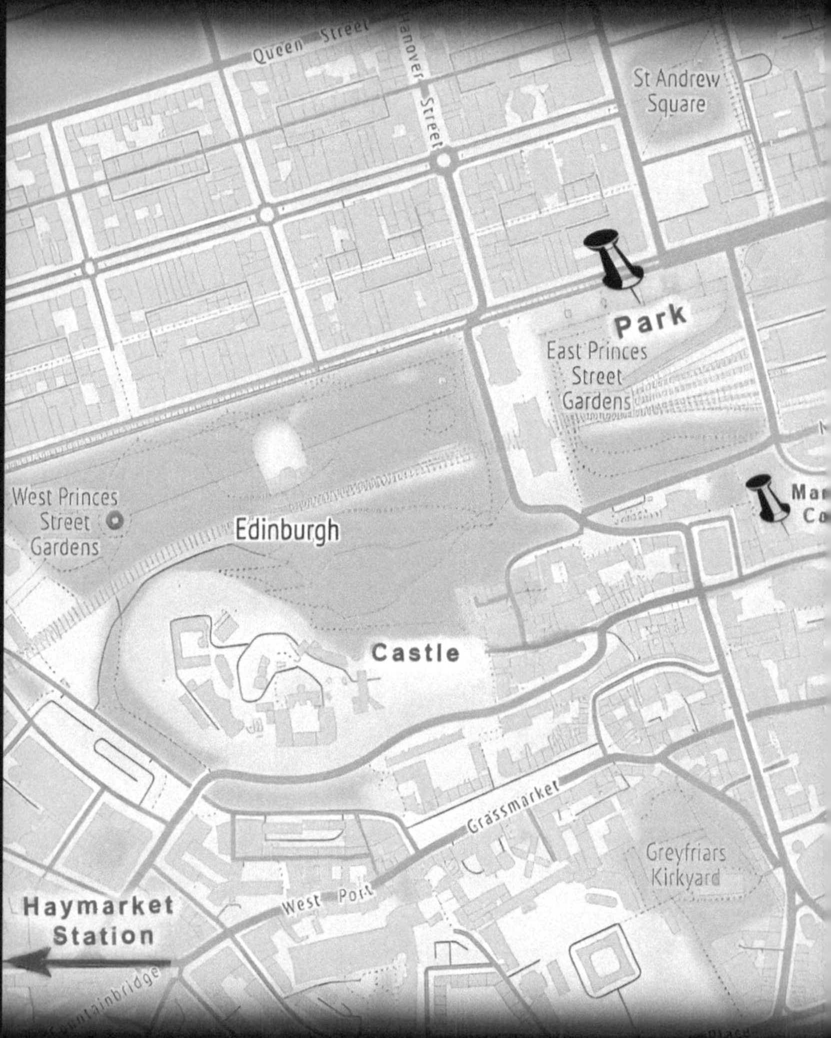

Queen Street
Hanover Street
St Andrew Square
Park
East Princes Street Gardens
West Princes Street Gardens
Edinburgh
Man
Ca
Castle
Grassmarket
Greyfriars Kirkyard
West Port
Haymarket Station
Fountainbridge
Place

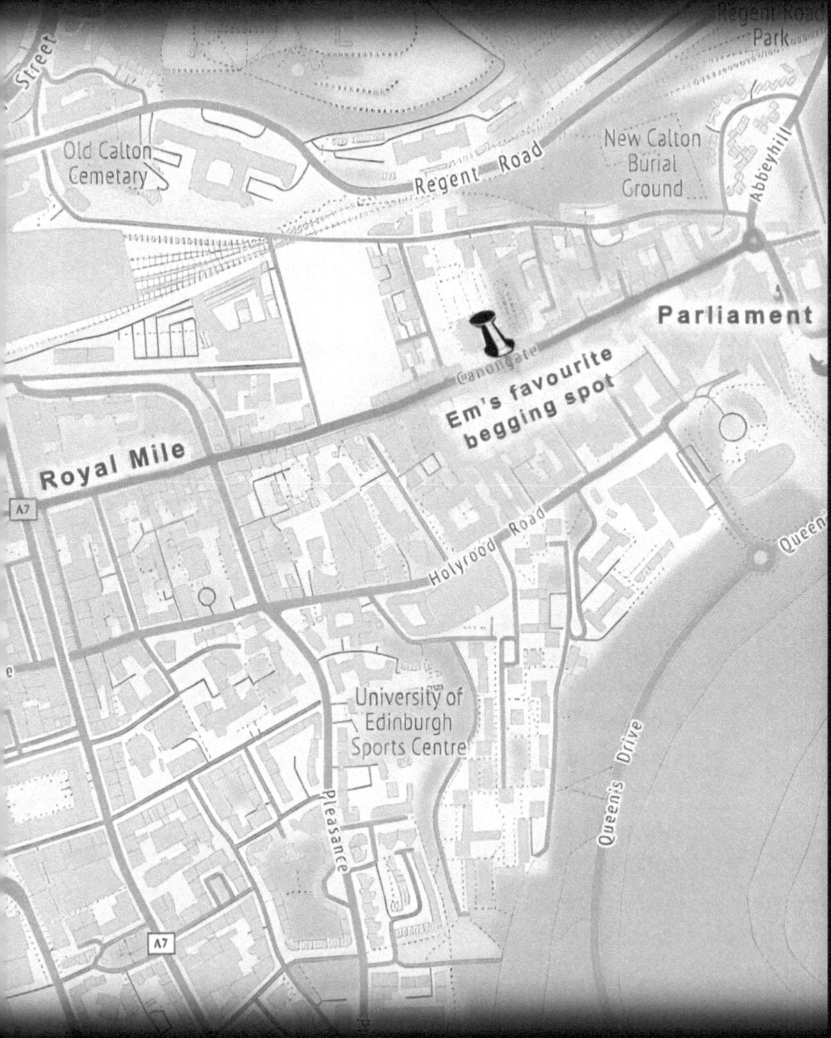

Street
Regent Road Park
Old Calton Cemetary
Regent Road
New Calton Burial Ground
Abbeyhill
Parliament
Canongate
Em's favourite begging spot
Royal Mile
A7
Holyrood Road
Queen's
University of Edinburgh Sports Centre
Pleasance
Queen's Drive
A7

# Contents

*Dedicated to chocolate.*
*You, sweet lady, help me write.*

# Before we begin

This book is set in Edinburgh, Scotland and is therefore written in British English.

Here are some words that are different on the other side of the pond:

**Close** - a very narrow street

**Flat** – apartment

**Hob** – cooker

**Laird** - lord (Scottish)

**Lass** - girl (Scottish)

**Mobile phone** – cell phone

**Nibbles** - snacks

**Quid** - pound (money)

**Telly** - television

**Tesco** - supermarket chain

**Wee** - small (Scottish)

Subscribe to Skye's newsletter and get a free book as a thank you: **skyemackinnon.com/newsletter**

# One

I was riding my girlfriend's strap-on when she told me to move out.

Six weeks later, I'm living on the streets. I wish we'd split up in the summer. Edinburgh in winter is fucking cold. There's no snow, but the icy wind is blowing straight through my thin trench coat. Oh yes, did I mention my ex also threw away all my stuff when I didn't collect it immediately? Hell, I didn't have anywhere to live yet, I was staying at friends' houses mostly. There was no space to put a dozen cardboard boxes. So, she threw it out without telling me. Bitch.

I don't even know why we were still together. I should have moved out ages ago. I guess it became a habit, living together, her paying the rent, me paying for everything else. Sleeping together. Fighting. Hurting. Bruising, occasionally.

Now I'm without a girlfriend, without a flat, without a job. At the beginning, I took my laptop to cafes and pubs to use their free Wi-Fi but, after a while, the money

I spent on drinks was more than the money I earned with my freelance translating. It's a dead job. Nowadays, people use the internet to translate their stuff. And the quick birth certificate translations I get through the agency don't pay enough to survive on. Now my laptop is at my friend Ali's house, where I stayed for a week until her parents came for a visit. For a whole fucking month. I should be grateful that I could sleep on her sofa for as long as I did, but it hurts that I'm now sitting on a cold park bench while my friends are in their flats and houses, warm, cosy, happy.

My two other friends here in Edinburgh are saying that I could stay with them again, but one of them's got a baby and no space, and the other has OCD. I stayed at her place for a night, but I saw how stressful it was for her to have someone else in her sanctuary, so I wouldn't want to do that to her again.

I should have made more friends. Three friends, that's all I've got. My girlfriend didn't like me spending time with other people, especially women. She was always the jealous type but, at the beginning, I found it endearing. It made me feel special. Now, I wish I'd seen those signs for what they were. I should have left her long ago, on my terms, with a new place to live sorted out and a moving van to take my stuff there. Instead, the opposite happened. She threw me out and now I'm lost, drifting while trying to find my feet.

Maybe I'll get a place in the hostel tonight. I sigh and watch my breath slowly disappear into the morning air. The sun is trying to break through the hanging clouds and its meek light is touching the frosty grass around me.

I'm in the centre of town, on a strip of park running right along busy Princes Street. From here, I can see the old town, its tall stone houses that huddle together on the volcanic rock, leading up to the imposing castle at one end and down to the parliament on the other. It's a beautiful view, one that every tourist captures when they come here. Even now, early in the morning, they are everywhere, conquering the city for themselves, outnumbering the locals on their way to work.

A fine mist covers the city, but it's not raining. Yet. It's true what they say about Scottish weather. It's terrible. It makes you really appreciate the sun when it can be bothered to shine a little. At the moment, it's still fighting for dominance with the clouds. Maybe later.

I watch people hurry by me, not sparing me a second glance. Dark coats, gloves, and in the case of the less fashion-conscious, woollen hats. They're all dressed for winter, even though they'll soon be in their warm offices, working away like the busy bees they are. I've never been one to work nine to five, but right now, I crave it. Better than sitting here, not doing anything.

I sigh and get up, shaking my frozen legs. Maybe sitting on a cold bench wasn't the best idea. But there are not enough tourists here yet to make begging worth it.

I hate it. I fucking hate it. Never thought I'd be begging for money. I've got a university degree – which also got me into debt, so there are no savings that could carry me over.

I have an overdraft, debts and no cash whatsoever. I thought about selling my laptop, but it's the only way I might still be able to find work again. For now, begging is the only way to survive. Two quid is enough to get me a few hours' warmth in a café with a hot drink. Luckily, they let me in, unlike some of the other rough sleepers. I don't look homeless yet, and hopefully I don't smell it either. I give my armpits a doubtful sniff. Could be worse. The church I stayed at last night didn't have a shower, but if I get a space in the hostel, I'll be able to have a quick one tonight. Using their totally masculine smelling menthol shampoo. But I'm not one to be choosy right now. Even if I smell like a fifty-year-old guy with dandruff.

At the hostel, I'll also get to give my clothes a quick wash. I've got a few more tops and one pair of jeans stored with Ali, but I'm trying to keep them for when my current ones start falling apart. I'm planning long term now. At the beginning, I thought it would only be a night or two until I'd find somewhere to stay. But then I missed an appointment with the council because the bus broke down, and now they're not seeing me as a priority. They told me I could move in with my parents again. Yeah, as if that's going to happen. They threw me out when I was sixteen, so I don't think they'd be pleased to take me in now. Maybe they won't even notice if I don't call them for Christmas this year. I'm certainly not going to spend any money on phoning them if I could spend it on a hot chocolate.

A drop of rain lands on my cheek. The sun has lost its battle. I better move, otherwise all the sheltered spots will be gone. Beggars *can* be choosy.

I grab my backpack, grimace at the dirt it's covered in,

and head towards the Royal Mile, where it's easiest to get noticed by tourists.

I keep my head down. I pretend I'm not, but I'm ashamed.

I find a spot in a covered archway close to the parliament. There are not many tourists here yet – most go to the Castle first before they head down to Holyrood Palace and the parliament – but sometimes the politicians and civil servants like to do a good deed on their way to work and give me a few pennies. That's what I learned straight away: the richer the person in front of me, the less they will put into my bowl. They only do it to feel virtuous, like the good samaritans they certainly are not.

The rain is getting heavier and a few drops find their way onto my clothes, but it's not bad enough yet to venture away from the Royal Mile. This is the most lucrative spot in the entire city. I grimace. Lucrative, what a strange word to use. It's almost like I'm looking at the begging like a business, but that's just wrong. This is only to carry me over until I get my next council appointment and hopefully end up on their list of emergency accommodation. I still can't believe they're not giving me any support. I always thought that people living on the streets only had themselves to blame. That they didn't want help or couldn't be bothered to ask for assistance. Now, my opinion on that has changed. I want help, but nobody is giving it to me, no matter how much I ask for it. I shudder when I remember the cold, uncaring eyes of the woman at the council. She didn't care that my bus had broken down. She didn't care that I had nowhere to go. She just gave me an appointment and made me feel like I should be grateful to only have to wait for six weeks. She's probably sitting in her cosy office just now, looking forward to going home tonight and relaxing in her warm living room. Meanwhile, I'll be freezing my arse off, unless I get a spot in the hostel. In the discarded newspaper I found yesterday, it mentioned snow being expected for the coming days.

More hostels and churches offer beds for the homeless during the winter, but there's still not enough spaces. Someone always has to stay outside, and it's been me several times already. At the beginning, I tried to be nice and let older people move in front of me in the queue, but that altruism is waning quickly. After a sleepless night on a park bench, a grateful smile from a little old lady does nothing to make me warm again. Or dry.

I wrap my arms around my chest, making myself a smaller target for the cold wind that's started to push through the archway. It's a wind channel. Great. No wonder there was nobody else sitting here already.

I peek up at the sky. Dark clouds are gathering above me. I'm not sure if I should be hoping for rain or for snow. Both make the ground wet. Both bring cold that will seep into my bones. I'd love me some sun, but right now, all I can hope for is that these clouds will pass, driven away by Edinburgh's strong sea winds.

Someone drops coins into my bowl and I hurry to look up and smile, but they've already disappeared into the crowd. Good. I hate looking at the people who give me money. They make me feel naked, exposed, dirty. I much prefer for them to stay anonymous.

I lean forward and check the bowl. Not coins. Stones. They actually threw tiny pebbles in there!

My cheeks heat in indignation. As if it wasn't humiliating enough to sit out here in the cold, no, someone thinks it's funny to put rocks in my bowl. I take them out, revealing the three one pound coins already in there. Two of them are from yesterday. I always try and keep some money behind so it looks as if people have thrown money in my bowl. Somehow, that makes other people add to it. Some kind of weird psychology, I guess, but it also makes me feel better, even though I know that it's not new money.

Three pounds. That's going to buy me a sandwich and a hot tea later on, unless I'm responsible and keep two coins for tomorrow. Then, I'll not even have enough for a coffee.

I grimace and continue to look at the sea of legs rushing past me. They're all full of purpose, rushing towards work or to go sightseeing, who knows? But they all have a destination. I don't. All I can do is sit here and hope that someone will be kind enough to give me a few pennies.

My stomach growls. Fuck. It's going to be a long day.

Two polished leather shoes stop in front of me. I look up – and straight at the crotch of the guy bending down to me. I look away, trying to hide an embarrassed smile. This is as close to a guy as I've come in years. My ex was the jealous type. Which is why I only have three good friends left, all the others let themselves be bullied away. Good riddance. And male friends were taboo – she knew I was bisexual, not just into women like herself, so she saw them as a threat. When I spoke with a guy at a party... not pretty.

"Why are you here?" he asks, and I stare at him.

"What do you think? This piece of pavement feels particularly nice, so I decided to sit here for a few hours."

He sits down next to me, hugging his long legs.

"You're right, this is quite comfortable."

I snort. This guy is crazy. If I could, I'd get up and walk away, but this spot has a roof and a steady stream of people. It's too good to abandon because of a random weirdo.

"What do you want?" I snarl at him, trying to look as unfriendly as possible. Please leave, I've got enough craziness of my own to deal with.

"Nothing, just taking a break. Walking up the hill is exhausting."

I give him a doubtful look. He's fit, I can tell even though he's wearing a thick leather jacket. There's no way this is guy out of breath from a little stroll up the hill. Edinburgh is full of hills, so if you live here, you get used to it.

"Please, go away," I try more politely this time.

"Why? You haven't answered my question yet."

"Ehm, what?"

"I asked why you're here, and sorry, but this really isn't comfortable." He shifts and his shoulder touches mine in the process. I shiver. Human touch has become a rarity in my life.

"Are you like a street pastor?"

He laughs. "Nah, I don't do God."

I breathe a sigh of relief. I wasn't in the mood for a sermon about what a sinful woman I am, thank you very much. I've had a few of that kind of people try and talk to me over the past weeks. When they offer that I can sleep in their churches for a night, I go with them, endure their speeches, trying to get done with it as soon as possible. If they only want to talk about God without offering me a place to sleep, I tell them to fuck off. Works most of the time.

"If you haven't noticed, I'm homeless. So if you don't want to throw something in my bowl, please move on. You're distracting."

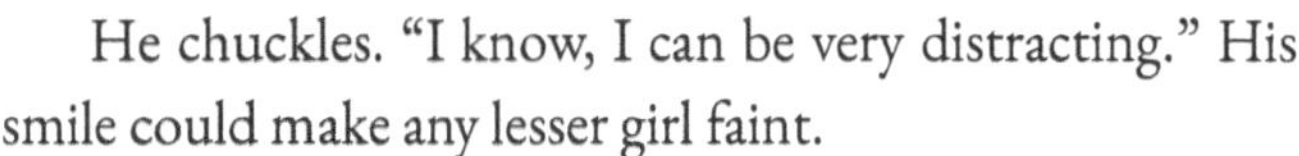

He chuckles. "I know, I can be very distracting." His smile could make any lesser girl faint.

I snort. "Sorry, wrong word. I meant annoying. Now piss off."

"You know you're not very polite?"

"Why should I be? You're invading my privacy."

"If I throw something in your bowl, will you come and get a coffee with me?"

Tempting, but that's creepy. This guy is too friendly. And that usually means trouble. My trust in humanity has suffered a lot since my first night on the streets. Some people think that just because you've got breasts, you're for sale. Or happy to be touched.

"I told you to piss off."

"Come on, it's freezing out here and I really don't want to sit on the cold pavement anymore. I'm in the mood for an americano and a piece of cake. Doesn't that tempt you?"

"I don't go with random men who I don't know," I reply, giving him an evil stare, which he apparently finds amusing.

"Then we better get to know each other." He holds out a gloved hand. "My name is Ben, pleased to meet you."

I don't make any move to take his hand, but he keeps it there, outstretched.

"Go away, Ben," I sigh, but he stays in the same position, grinning like he's the funniest person in the world. The most desperate, maybe. He twitches his fingers, wiggling them one by one.

"Is it the glove that's bothering you? I can take it off."

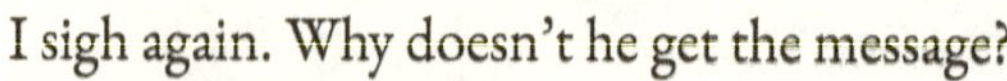

I sigh again. Why doesn't he get the message?

He takes off his glove and I cringe. His hand is covered in scars, big, fleshy ones. One disappears under the sleeve of his jumper, tempting me to follow it. A silent vulnerability has crept into his eyes, making me think twice about refusing again.

I shake his hand. "I'm Em."

"M, like the letter?"

"Em, like Emily."

"Nice to meet you, Em. Now, how about that coffee?"

"I don't drink coffee. I'm a tea person."

"Tea it is." He gets up and offers me his now gloved hand. I'm about to refuse when I realise I need the loo. Using the toilet in a café beats the public ones by miles. I take his hand and he pulls me up. I sway a little; after sitting in the cold for so long, my feet are frozen. He reaches out to steady me, but I evade him and jump up and down a little, causing him to smile. I stop and glare at him, until he tries to hide his grin.

"There's this cute little coffee shop just around the corner, I go there a lot to work." He points at his messenger bag, bulging with papers and a large laptop.

"What do you do?" I ask, unable to stifle my curiosity.

"This and that," he replies mysteriously. "I can tell you about it in the café."

"You're very persistent, you know that, right?"

"Oh, my flatmates tell me every day."

Flatmates? He looks like he's in his mid-thirties and

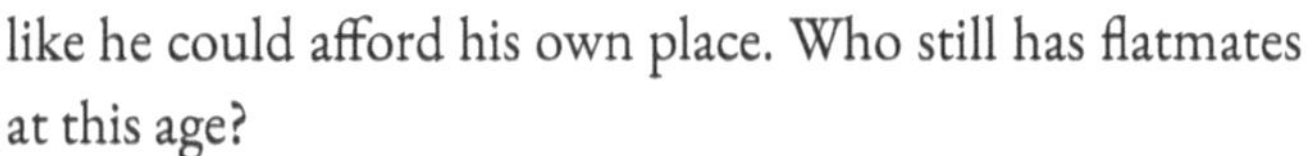

like he could afford his own place. Who still has flatmates at this age?

We start walking down the Royal Mile, trying to avoid the groups of tourists huddled together at street corners, listening to their shouting guides.

After a moment of silence, I ask the question that's been hovering on my tongue.

"You have flatmates?"

"Yes, two. Alistair inherited a house and invited us to stay for a summer. It's been four years now, and still working well."

"Don't you want to live on your own?" I loved having my own little flat before I moved in with Jess. Right now, I wish I had somewhere to stay. Even just a room, as long as it was my own, and not shared with crowds of other homeless folks.

"It's a large house, so we can stay out of each other's way if we want, but at the same time, if I want company, I don't need to go far to find it. And this way I don't have to spend a lot of money on rent that I could spend on other things."

"Like what?"

He grins. "Right now, coffee."

He holds open the door of a small café that I almost didn't notice. It's in one of the narrow closes leading off the Royal Mile, one of the darker ones that I wouldn't usually walk through at night. The café looks very inviting though. Candles flicker on the small iron wrought tables, comfy cushions cover the sofas and chairs dotted around the room. And the best thing: it's warm. Roasting, actually.

"May I take your coat?" Ben asks, and I indulge him and let him take it off my shoulders. Apparently, he's got some kind of good Samaritan complex.

He even pulls back my chair when I sit down. A real gentleman. And I still don't know what he wants from me. That worries me more than I want to admit. I hate not knowing.

He orders our drinks from an old lady standing behind a row of cakes and scones, and then sits down opposite me, staring straight into my eyes. I can't help but stare back.

"Have you ever stolen something?" he asks suddenly.

"No," I say automatically before even wondering why he's asking me that question.

"Truth. Interesting."

"Why is that interesting? Not everyone living on the streets is a criminal."

"Obviously." He leans forwards, his elbows pressed on the white table cloth, his index fingers touching his chin. I feel like an animal in the zoo, being stared at curiously. Or, maybe more accurately, a gazelle being ogled by a lion.

"What do you want, Ben?" I sigh, evading his intense brown eyes.

"To get to know you."

"You know, this is really creepy. I think I should go." I move to get up, but the old woman bringing our drinks is in the way.

"Leaving already, dearie?" I look at her tray and see hot chocolate. And sit back down. If it had been tea, I might have been able to leave, but now there's no chance in hell. Hot chocolate is heaven in a mug. With whipped cream on top.

"No, just looking for the toilets."

"Just around the corner, love." I nod my thanks and follow her directions to a sliding door hiding a single same-sex toilet. I breathe out deeply when I'm finally on my own again, away from Ben. He's strange. Good-looking, almost hot, but very, very strange. I don't get a read on him, and I'm usually good at reading people. He's too friendly. Normally, when people are this friendly, they want something in return. He doesn't look like the type who has to pay for sex. I mean, look at him. He'd just have to chat up a random girl at a party to get a quick fuck, or two. So why is he talking to me? A dirty, unnoticeable street rat?

I take my sweet time, washing my face in the small sink and rubbing some soap on my armpits. Deodorant, Em style. My brown hair is sticky and filthy. I run my hands through it a few times, trying to get the knots out of it. I should probably cut it short, that's more practical for the life I'm currently living. Conditioning my hair is not very high on my list of priorities. My bra is itchy and I'd love to wash it, but I don't want to go back not wearing it. It feels safer with it on, somehow, especially with my shirt being such a thin one.

After another splash of water on my face to wash away the last of the grime, I return to Ben and my hot chocolate. The cream on top of it has started to melt a little, so it's the first thing on my plan of attack. I scoop it up and devour it, savouring the taste of cocoa-covered cream.

Ben watches me with an amused twinkle in his eyes as I delight in slurping the chocolaty foam hiding beneath the cream. I have to come here again, this is the best hot chocolate I've had in years. Then I look at the price written on the large board above the counter and decide not to. At least, not while I still live on the streets. Once I'm back on my own two feet and have a regular income again, I'll come here every day.

I try and pace myself, but suddenly, my mug is empty and Ben is trying to hide a laugh.

"Mary, could we have another hot chocolate, please? Add some marshmallows this time."

Maybe he isn't as bad as I thought at first. I stare at my empty mug, watching tiny brown air bubbles pop their final goodbye on the white porcelain.

"Do you lie?" Ben suddenly asks and I lift my head to stare at him incredulously.

"Seriously? Why are you asking me stuff like that when you could be asking me for my sob story?"

"You didn't answer me when I asked you about that earlier," he says softly.

"Yes, I lie. Not more than everyone else, though. I think."

"Are you a good liar?"

"I guess? It's not something to be proud of, so I've not given it much thought."

He nods. "Let's play a game. Give me three statements about yourself, two truths and one lie, and I'll try and tell them apart."

"No, you start." I don't want to be branded a liar by him.

"Feisty, I like it." He takes a sip from his Americano, which must now surely be cold. "I had a poodle called Mr Fluffy. My favourite colour is black. I have a license to carry a gun."

"The third one."

"Wrong. My favourite colour is pink."

I snort-gasp. "Seriously? That was a second lie."

"Is it?" He smiles mysteriously. "Your turn."

"Okay, let me think. I've never taken drugs. I used to do ballet." I flash my teeth. "I had a Labrador called Mrs Wiggle."

He laughs at the last one. Good. If they laugh, they are more likely to think it's a lie. His smile disappears and he begins to study me, his face suddenly serious.

"Interesting..." he mutters under his breath, but we get interrupted by the woman he called Mary, who's bringing me my second hot chocolate. This time, she's put a heap of tiny marshmallows on the saucer. Perfect. I don't like it when they get soggy.

"The last one," he says confidently.

"Wrong, she really was called that."

"Then the first."

I huff. "Just because I live on the streets doesn't mean that I take drugs, or steal, or lie. This is becoming quite insulting. I never did ballet, I'm not a girly girl, nor have I ever been. I did kickboxing instead."

"Wow, that's unexpected. And useful."

"Useful for what?"

"Mary, could we have some cake?" he calls out instead of answering.

She shuffles over to our little table. "Which one would

you like, dearie?" He raises an eyebrow at being called that, but gives her an indulgent smile.

"The raspberry gateau you had last week was delicious. I don't suppose..."

She chuckles. "I've got some in the fridge. I save it for my special customers. And what would you like, darling?"

I look over at the display case filled with the most delicious cakes. "Something with chocolate?"

Ben laughs. "Do you eat anything besides chocolate?"

"Not if I don't have to," I shoot back, my eyes drawn to the large piece of chocolate cake Mary is now placing on a plate.

"Cream?" she asks and I don't find words to reply to this amazing woman.

"Yes, she wants cream," Ben answers her with a chuckle.

Mary takes a glass bowl covered with cling film out of the fridge and reveals a massive portion of whipped cream. Not the cheap bottle stuff, no, the good, fatty, calorific goodness. She puts a generous scoop on my giant piece of cake. I think I'm in heaven.

When Mary puts the plate in front of me, I'm experiencing a food orgasm. Ben looks like he's having fun watching me, but I don't let that deter me from my feast. While he is taking his sweet time with his gateau, my chocolate cake is disappearing at an alarming speed. I will have to brush my teeth extra carefully tonight. The thought of using the public toilets near the station almost drives away my appetite. At night, they are not a place you'd want to be. Smelly, creepy, dark.

"What else do you like besides chocolate?" Ben asks me when I'm finally slowing down a bit.

"Carrots. Spinach. Walnuts." I reply in between chewing on a piece of dark chocolate that found its way into the sponge.

"I didn't mean food, but that's good to know."

"You didn't specify. What food do you like?"

"Sushi," he grins, knowing that I won't be able to resist questioning that.

"But sushi doesn't have chocolate in it. Or is there chocolate sushi?"

"I think you're going to get hyper from all that sugar. Has nobody told you it's not healthy to eat so much sweet stuff?"

"I told you, I also like carrots."

"Which are sweet," he retorts.

"Spinach isn't."

"Okay, spinach is healthy. But you shouldn't eat too much of it, it's got a lot of iron in it."

He looks at me so seriously that I break out in laughter.

"You're not my dietician, so you can piss off."

"Language," he chides and I gape at him.

"Seriously?"

"Seriously," he confirms. "Alistair won't tolerate swearing in his house."

"Well, guess it's good then that I'm not living in his house."

"I was going to-" He breaks off as his phone vibrates in his breast pocket. He checks the caller info and sighs. "I need to take this, wait here."

He goes outside, leaving his jacket behind. It's cold, he'll be freezing. Hopefully it's not a long call. He's walking back and forth, talking agitatedly. I wait a few minutes, sipping the last of my hot chocolate. Then I remember that I still don't know what he wants from me and that it's not safe, so I take my stuff, slip into my coat and sprint out of the cafe while he has his back turned. I hope Mary didn't think I'd stolen anything. Running away probably made me suspicious.

Ben turns when he hears the little bells hanging behind the door, but it's too late, I'm already halfway up the close. I didn't tell him, but I used to be in the running team at school. I'm fast and, right now, I'm running as fast as I can.

# Three

It's a cold night, but luckily, it's one I get to spend inside a warm dorm room at a hostel - courtesy of Ben. After I left him at the café, I found a twenty-pound note in my coat pocket - the sneaky bastard must have put it there while I was on the toilet. By now, I'm no longer too proud to reject help. Instead, I'm staying in the cheapest hostel I can find, surrounded by tourists giving me curious stares. I'm the only one who doesn't have a large backpack or suitcase with me, and my clothes have suffered over the past few weeks. I wash them in the shared bathroom before taking a long, delicious shower, washing away the grime and worries of the day. There's even some coconut shampoo a traveller must have left behind. I delight in the smell and new softness of my hair. For once, it's got a bit of its old shine back.

The dorm room is noisy, but I'm used to much worse and it doesn't bother me. Not in the slightest. I sleep better than I have in weeks, almost without nightmares.

I stay until 11am when I have to check out, taking

advantage of the free tea and toast. A few slices of bread find their way into my backpack, for later. It's not stealing, I paid for it. Well, Ben did.

I wonder what he's doing now. He's probably forgotten about me already; I certainly hope so. I've got a weird feeling about him. He was too nice. People aren't nice without wanting something in return. And it's usually pretty clear what they want. Company. Favours. Sex. But with him... I just can't understand his motives. And I ran away before I could find out - which was probably the safest option.

I step out into the cold winter air. It's time to earn my living. I make my way back to the Royal Mile, drawn in by the tourists flocking here. There will be more once the fake German Christmas market starts, but it's already quite a lot. To be honest, there are always tourists in Edinburgh, no matter the time of year. Most of them ignore beggars but, as a young woman, I've got more chances of getting some coins than the older men usually lingering on street corners. People seem to pity me. I hate it.

My usual spot is taken, so I walk down towards the parliament, looking for a place that's got some protection from the cold wind that's starting to pick up. There's a shop not far that has a grate in front of it which exudes hot exhausts - and bingo, there's nobody there. Gratefully, I sink down on the warm metal, getting my bowl out of my backpack. Somehow, people expect there to be a hat. I tried a hat, but a bowl seems to work better.

Just when I've found a comfortable position,

someone clears their throat from behind me. "Move, please, we don't want your kind around here."

The shopkeeper is a large man with thick hands that are clutching a souvenir tea towel featuring Nessie. I stare at it, mesmerised by the contrast of something so trivial and the painful words the man just said.

"Go on, you're putting off my customers."

Swallowing a heated response, I get up and walk down the street, not looking back. I don't want him to see the shame on my flushed face.

♥

I find a sheltered spot below a stone gate leading to an alleyway off the main street. It's not as visible but, right now, I want to be invisible anyway. It's days like these where I am most aware of what I have lost and what I have become.

It's another two weeks until my next Council appointment to find out if I get emergency accommodation. Another fortnight on the streets. It's getting colder every day, and who knows how long it'll take for them to find me somewhere temporary to stay. If they offer me something at all. I curse my ex for getting me into this situation, but in the end, the only person I have to be angry at is me. I was the one making her angry. I didn't manage to get a full-time job because I chose the wrong thing to study. I'm the one who insisted on having a social life rather than try and earn more money during university, which is why I now have debts. I'm the one who missed my Council appointment. I should have taken an earlier bus. I should have tried harder to persuade Jess to let me stay, no matter the cost. It couldn't have got much worse, and I was used to it. Better than staying on the streets, surely.

The sound of pound coins landing in my bowl rips me out of my thoughts. I look up to smile at the generous person - and frown instead as I see Ben. Damn, I should have chosen somewhere else to beg today. Edinburgh is a big city, there would have been enough other opportunities. But I had to be greedy and go back to the Mile.

"Fancy seeing you here, Emily," he says sarcastically.

"It's Em. Now piss off."

He clucks his tongue. "That's no way to thank someone for their donation."

"Fine, thanks for the money. You can take it and leave."

He sighs and turns to leave, but then falters. "Would you like another hot chocolate?"

"No. I don't trust you. Leave me the fuck alone." I hope this spelled it out enough for him.

"Okay," he says softly, "I'll go."

This time, he doesn't turn back, leaving me with five one-pound coins and the taste of guilt in my mouth.

❤

His money buys me a sandwich in the reduced section at Tesco's and a hot tea. The rest I keep for my dinner. It should be enough for a soup somewhere to dispel the cold from my bones.

Once I've devoured the sandwich, I head to Haymarket station. I'm sure I won't cross paths with Ben here, it's quite a bit away from the Royal Mile. And maybe the commuters will give me enough to buy me another night in a hostel. Otherwise I'll try one of the churches that open for winter. I shudder at the thought of listening to the priest's sermon again. The last church I stayed at, we had to take part in a service before we were given some food. Once you've lived on the streets for a bit, any belief you ever had in a God or in humanity disappears. I've seen people do things that I would never have thought I'd see while I was still living my ordinary life. Stuff that you usually only see on the telly or in the news. And the stories you hear... every single one of them could be made into a book or a film. Loss, abuse, misfortune, bankruptcy. Sometimes stupidity, but that is probably very arrogant coming from me.

Haymarket is busy as usual. It will be even busier in a few hours when the commuters leave the city, and others return. There's a kiosk in front of the station which sells hot drinks and I'm tempted to get myself a tea to warm my frozen hands, but I need to save my money for tonight. Better cold now than sleeping on an empty stomach. I walk around the corner, away from any police or station security, and look for a spot on the ground that doesn't look like a few dozen dogs have already marked it today. I used to like dogs. Not anymore.

I sit down and go to work.

♥

Four hours later, darkness has fallen and the last commuters are leaving the station, too tired to even look at me. It's time to go. There's a church not far from here, and I know that even if it is closed, there'll be a poster with the schedule of which church is open tonight. They open at least one church to the homeless each night during the winter, something I didn't know until I was on the streets. I hope it's one in the city centre; I don't feel like walking through the cold and the dark for too long.

It only takes me a few minutes, but the nearest church is closed and there's no poster in the display box by the gate. Fuck. Some idiot must have taken it. I rack my brain about where the next church is. I've lived in this city for a long time, but it's not as if I know every damn church in this area. I was never really interested in them until I became homeless. Now, they're my only hope of a warm and safe bed for the night. I guess I could try one of the hostels, but they're usually full by now. I count my money. Seven pounds, forty-two pence. Enough for dinner and breakfast, and maybe lunch, at a stretch. Not enough to pay for somewhere to stay.

I walk back to Haymarket and head straight to the tram stop. There's a map at the shelter, showing the nearest tram and bus stops - and other churches. Most of them look too small or are not the right denomination, but there's one maybe fifteen minutes away, in one of the parts of town that I don't like walking through at night. Too many dark corners and unsavoury characters. Oh well, it can't be helped. I can see my breath in the frosty air; it's going to be freezing tonight. I don't even have a sleeping bag anymore, that was stolen after one of my first few nights on the streets. I was gullible back then, naive, thinking that everybody who smiles was nice. Well, lesson learned.

Bracing myself against the cold wind, drawing my hood deep over my face, I walk through the night, leaving the bright station behind me. The space between the street lamps gets ever bigger the further I walk. I'm no longer in a residential area where I feel almost safe at night.

"Lass, got a few quid for me?" a rasping voice suddenly asks and I almost jump. I can't make out much in the darkness, but the man looks to be in his fifties, and even wrapped in his coat I can see how thin he is. He steps forward and in the pale light of a street lamp his face is skeletal, his eyes sunken and dull. A junkie, most likely. Someone to stay far away from.

"Got nothing for ya, mate," I drawl in my best street voice. My slightly posh English accent made me a target at the beginning, so now I've learned to hide it. I'm not sure I'm doing a good job of it. Even though I've lived in Edinburgh for years, I've never quite got rid of my English accent.

"Sleeping rough, lass?" he asks, coming closer at the same time as I'm stepping back.

"Aye, need to be on my way. See ya around," I reply politely and turn. A second later, I'm on the ground, screaming in pain, my ankle hurting like hell from where it slipped off the curb. "Fuck!" I shout, not caring about who hears me.

I drag myself off the street before I'm run over by a

car, wincing at every movement of my ankle. If it's not broken, it's definitely sprained. Just what I needed.

"Fuck," I curse again, before becoming aware of the thin guy approaching me. He's suddenly got a swagger to him that makes me afraid.

"Did you say you had some money for me?" he rasps, bending down until his face is level with mine. His teeth are yellow and his breath stinks of something that reminds me of stale garlic. I want to get up and run away, but my ankle is sending waves of pain through me even when I just think of moving it.

"I don't have anything, I'm in the same boat as you."

"I don't believe you."

I'm starting to panic. His pupils are dilated; he's high. Reasoning with him isn't an option.

"A guy gave me something earlier, but I've only got six quid left." I rummage in my pockets, pushing away the desperate voice in me shouting that this is my last money. Finally, I find the coins and show them to him, still somehow hoping that he'll believe me and leave.

"You think you can screw me over? Nah, lass, let me have a look, I'm sure you've got some more hidden away under your pretty coat."

He grabs me by the shoulders and pushes me onto my back. My ankle burns in agony as I try to fight him. The martial arts skills that I usually rely on require functioning limbs. I can't even knee him between the legs because my ankle can't carry the weight of the rest of my body. Fuck, fuck, fuck!

As he rips open my coat, I scream out for help. We're

not far from the station, there might be people around to hear me.

He mumbles something and suddenly there's something in my mouth, something scratchy and smelly. The bastard has gagged me. I struggle more, trying to get out of his grip. He's thin, but he is stronger than he looks.

I thrash, trying to wiggle out from under him somehow. He's kneeling on me, his knees pinning down my legs, his hands grabbing my own. I'm trying to spit out the gag; calling for help is my only chance of getting away from him. The hard asphalt is pressing against my spine, letting the cold seep into my body. I groan as he lifts my arms over my head, securing them with one hand, while fumbling with the buttons of my coat with the other. Despite my struggles, he manages to open the top two, and slides a hand inside, over the thin shirt I wear underneath. He's not looking for money now; he never even checked my coat pockets. He's after something else.

Where are all the people? It can't be later than eight, and while we are on a street with mostly businesses and warehouses, it's not like pedestrians never come here. We're close to the train station, people must walk along this road from time to time.

I twist my head, trying to see around me. That's when he puts his hand on my breast. I scream against the gag as he touches me, squeezes, scratches. His fingernails rake over my skin. It hurts so much that I think he must have drawn blood. With him busy leering at my upper body, I manage to get one hand free. I make a fist and slam it against his face - weak because of the angle, but enough for him to scream in surprise and let my other arm go.

With both arms free, I can finally do more than just lie on the ground like a helpless victim. I hit his cheek again at the same time as he grabs my hair and pulls. I squeal, but my fist meets its target and he lets go again, instinctively covering his face. I rip the gag out of my mouth and shout for help. My voice is hoarse, but loud enough to be heard. Please, please let there be someone walking nearby. Please.

My attacker is still sitting on top of my legs, and I know that even if I managed to get them free, I'd not be able to run with my ankle. Which means I need to knock him out before he gets the upper hand again. I make a flat hand and swing back for a blow to his windpipe, but he's faster and suddenly, his hands are around my throat, squeezing the life out of me. I can't breathe, and panic sits in as I see the crazed look in his eyes.

"You don't need to be conscious for this, lass," he whispers as he presses his fingernails into the soft skin on my neck. "Or alive."

I gasp for air, but there is none to be had. I've got my hands free, but his arms are longer and his face is just out of reach. I claw at his arms, but his coat is thick and I'm not sure he even notices it. Black spots cover the edges of my vision and a strange fog takes hold of my mind. I feel my limbs move, but I'm no longer able to control my motions. How the fuck did I get here, dying on a lonely street at night?

My eyelids flutter and the burn in my lungs ebbs away as I slowly drift off.

"What are you doing?" a voice shouts from a distance, and I can hear someone running towards us. "Police!"

Finally, I think, as the fog in my mind threatens to

pull me under. Maybe they're too late, but at least they'll catch the guy who killed me.

More people arrive and the pressure on my throat finally lessens. I try to breathe, but it hurts.

"Get an ambulance!" the same voice calls out, but suddenly I can feel hands on my neck again and I try to move to fight them off, but there is no strength left in me.

"Shhush, I'm just feeling your pulse, relax," someone says, and a moment later, one of my eyelids is pulled open, but I don't see anything. I don't even remember closing my eyes. Now that I'm no longer being suffocated, I try to breathe deeply, but my lungs won't do as they're told. I'm not getting enough air, no matter how much I gasp.

"Try and breathe slowly. The ambulance will be here any second now."

I wish I could just go to sleep. Unconsciousness, sleep, death, whatever. Everything hurts. I can't breathe. The sounds around me are painfully vibrating in my skull. They are becoming louder. More voices, cars, sirens. Things are happening around me, but I'm so tired.

"Stay with me, sweetheart, help is coming."

I don't want to. I want to sleep.

"What happened?"

"Strangulation. Pulse is 120 and weak. GCS eight. We've taken the suspect into custody".

They continue to talk, but I couldn't care less. When they start doing things to my body, I crawl further into myself, hiding from the pain and fear. I shiver inside, trembling as I make myself as small as I can. Please let the pain end.

# Four

"What's your name?"

"Emily Malone." My voice is hoarse and broken. Speaking hurts like hell. They've given me water to soothe my throat, but it's not helping much.

"Are there any next of kin you'd like us to call?"

"No," I whisper.

"Do you want to make your statement now or shall we come back later?"

I'm so grateful for that question that I want to hug the gentle police woman sitting by my bedside.

"Later," I croak, and with a soft squeeze of my shoulder, she leaves together with her colleague.

I try to sleep again, but the collar around my throat is itching and my ankle is pulsing painfully. The next time the nurse comes, I'll need to ask her for more painkillers. Maybe they will help dull my thoughts as well.

When I woke up a few hours ago, I was in a cloudy world, half dream, half reality. Nothing hurt, not even the memories. It was so peaceful. But the longer I was awake, the faster the clouds disappeared. Now I'm fully conscious, and I'm hating it. I don't want to feel.

I try reaching for the glass of water standing on the little bedside table, but my arms feel like lead, too weak to even lift off the mattress. There's nothing for me to do but stare at the ceiling.

♥

A knock on the door rips me from my doze. I turn my head, and inwardly curse the collar around my neck that is now painfully reminding me of its existence. And of what happened last night.

"Don't try to move," a soft voice chides me. It reminds me of someone but surely... Ben. He's here.

"How?" I ask, but it comes out as a croaking whisper.

He laughs sadly. "Didn't think I'd miss not being able to argue with you. But I guess now you'll just have to listen. Even if that's a little one-sided."

He drags a chair over and sits down, looking straight at me with his dark brown eyes. I want to turn away from their scrutiny, but this time I remember the collar and stay still.

"The police told me you were here."

The police? Why would they tell him?

Bastard. He knows I won't be able to ask questions, so why is he not giving me more information.

"How are you feeling?"

I shrug, not wanting to waste painful words on such a trivial question. I'm in hospital with a broken ankle, a bruised throat and a mind that replays the events of last night over and over again. I've been better.

"Water?" I whisper, trying to move as little as possible.

He takes the glass but instead of just holding it to my lips, he gently puts a hand behind my head and lifts me up slightly until I'm in a more comfortable position to drink. I take a few slow sips while he is patiently keeping me upright. When I'm done, he lowers me back onto the pillow, but his hand stays in place, cupping the back of my head, gently massaging my scalp.

"How?" I ask again, my voice a little stronger this time.

"After I walked away from you yesterday, I tried finding you again, but you had gone. I sent my contact in the police a message with your name and description, asking him to pass it on to his officers. I hadn't expected a call this soon, though." He frowns. "You shouldn't have run. You should have let me help you."

I grimace. "Why?"

"Why you should have accepted my help? Because then you wouldn't be here, you'd be safe at my place. You wouldn't have been all alone on the streets. You wouldn't have almost got killed... and raped."

He's almost shouting now. It reminds me of other shouting, last night, the hands on my throat, the fingers beneath my shirt. Fear floods my mind; I need to get away from him. I move despite my muscles being heavy and painful, rolling over, groaning as the collar presses against my bruises.

"Em, don't move," Ben says, a lot quieter, but no less emotional. "Please. Sorry I shouted, I get a little loud sometimes, I'm sorry. Please, don't move. I don't want you to hurt."

At the sound of his panicked voice, I stop my frenzied scramble. With a few quick steps, he's on the other side of the bed where I have made it to in my pitiful escape attempt. Now that he's looking at me with this vulnerable expression around his eyes, I notice that I wasn't scared of him. What I felt was the fear from earlier, amplified as a memory.

"It's okay," I whisper, exhaustion making it hard to speak.

He kneels on the floor so his eyes are on the same level as mine.

"I was so afraid when they called me. I know you won't believe me, and I don't expect you to, but... I don't know how to say it. I wanted you to be safe, and you weren't. I was scared that you were dead. Killed because you ran from me. Gone before I could tell you why I chose you."

"You chose me?" I croak. I would like to tell him that he's self-obsessed and that he doesn't need to feel guilty, but words hurt.

"There's a reason why I asked you to go to that cafe with me. Why it was important to talk to you." He sighs. "It just didn't go to plan."

I think he's waiting for an answer, but I just point to my throat instead of talking. He'll get the message.

"First, let's get you comfortable again."

He helps me back in my previous position, even fluffs the pillows beneath my head. When I'm lying comfortably again, he sits on the chair next to the bed and looks at me curiously.

"I didn't expect you to be this stunning."

"What?" Now he's lost me.

"When I read your profile, I imagined someone a little less... more ordinary. With your intelligence, I didn't hope for beauty as well. Not that I was hoping for you to be pretty. It doesn't matter. But..." He pauses. "I'm talking myself into a hole here, right?"

I nod, still completely confused by what he's trying to say. Intelligence? Pretty? Profile?

With his scarred hand, he wipes a strand of his black hair out of his face before looking into my eyes again. Why does he always do this? He's very intense.

"I was given your profile when I was looking for a possible assistant. There aren't many translators out there who speak Albanian, Italian and Russian. I had read through a few profiles and found them lacking a certain... extra, but when I came across yours, I wanted to know more. But in our work, we first need to do some research before contacting people. I was about to get in touch when you moved out of your partner's flat and didn't register a new one. I thought it was temporary, but you didn't reappear in the system until I saw an application for emergency housing. That's when you went up even higher on my list of possible candidates."

He pauses and notices me staring at him. Noticing my confusion, he sighs. "I can't tell you more until you sign a few documents. For now, think of me as someone who's offering you a job. A well-paid one with a range of benefits. Including free housing."

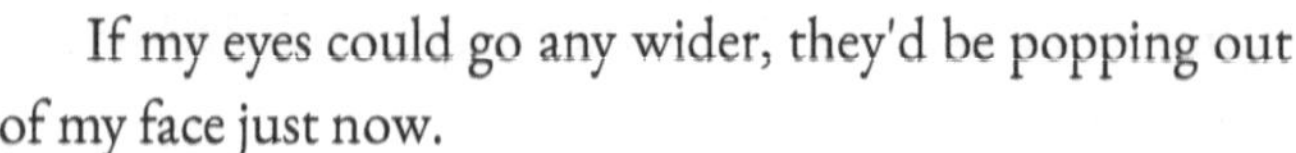

If my eyes could go any wider, they'd be popping out of my face just now.

"Not... a... whore," I croak, and his expression darkens.

"That's not what I meant. I know we got off to a bad start, but I'm hoping to make this right. Think about it: would I really go through all this trouble trying to contact you if all I wanted was a prostitute? Believe me, they are a lot easier to find than you were."

His phone vibrates in his pocket and he looks at his watch, frowning. "I need to leave soon. The doctors say you'll need to stay another night at least, and they won't release you until you have a place to stay. So, you can either wait for the Council to come up with a solution, or you can accept my offer. And with that I only mean the room, you don't need to commit yourself to the job yet."

"Where?" I ask, and he smiles.

"At the house I share with my colleagues. Friends, actually. There's a studio flat on the ground floor that's been empty for a while. You'll have your own kitchen and bathroom. It's small, but I hope it'll do for now until we find a more permanent solution."

I'm speechless. And sceptical. Maybe the mysterious 'job' he keeps talking about doesn't even exist. Maybe this is all just one big plan to hold me captive at his place. But no, that doesn't make any sense. If he's really gone through all this trouble just to find a homeless woman, there has to be more to it. I wish my brain was working properly, but it's still foggy from the painkillers. Not that they're working.

His phone vibrates again and he looks at it, irritation evident on his face.

"Sorry, I need to go. Do you need anything? A book perhaps, or some music?"

I shake my head and wince. I don't want to be in his debt, no matter how tempting the offer is. There's a little tv in this room, and once I find out where the remote is, that can be my entertainment for the day. Or even better, I could sleep.

"I'll come back tomorrow," he says and, almost as an afterthought, gently strokes my cheek. "Bye, Emily."

I frown at the gesture. He's behaving as if he's known me for ages, or is he always this familiar with strangers? He's already out of the door when I whisper, "Bye."

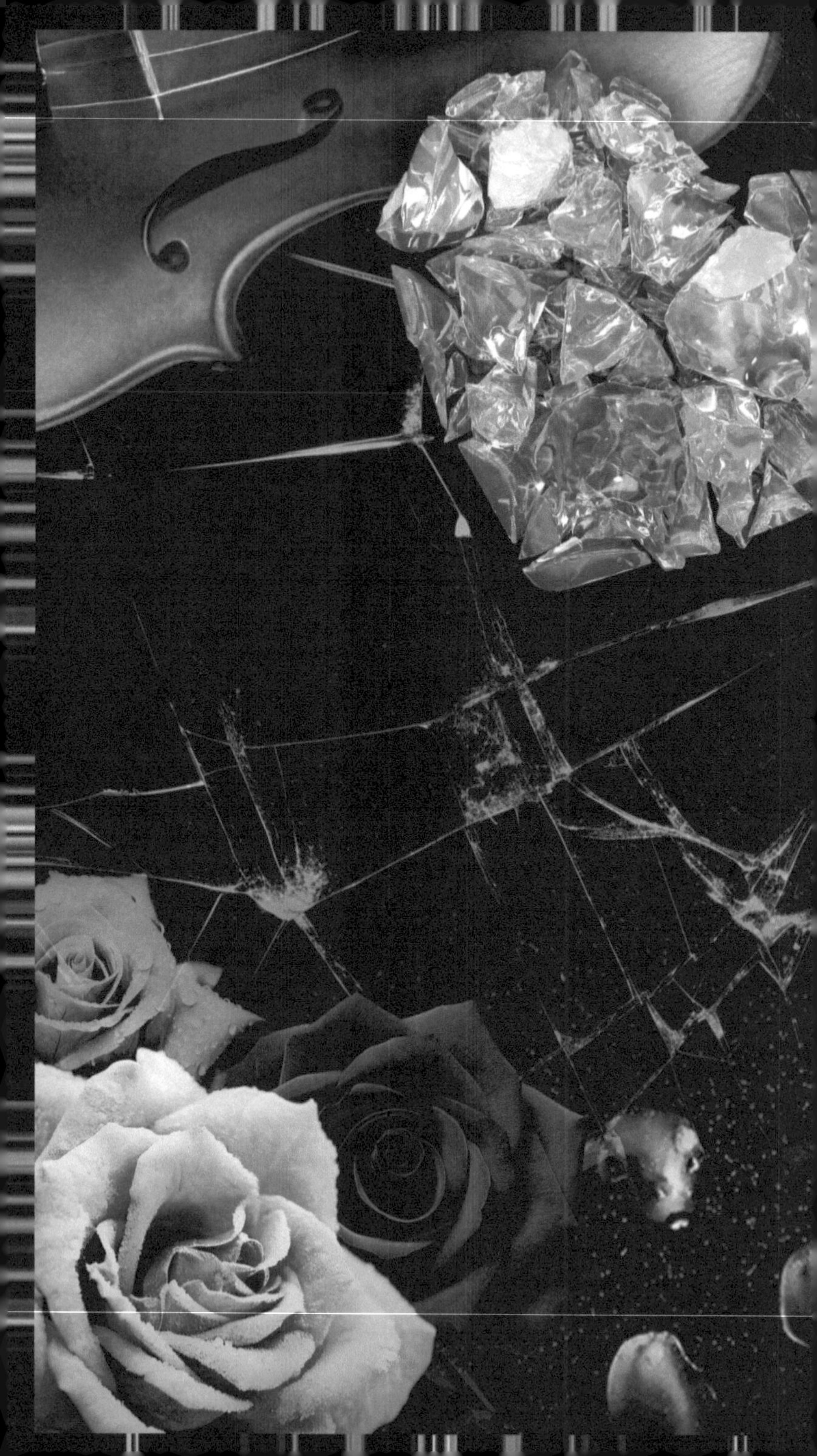

# Five

When I wake up, Ben is sitting by my bedside, eating ice cream. When he sees that I'm awake, he chuckles.

"Sorry, I actually bought this for you, but when you weren't awake, I thought it would be a waste for it to melt." He takes a second spoon from the bedside table. "It's better than grapes. Want some?"

I'm about to decline when he adds, "It's chocolate."

I smile, moving muscles that haven't been used for a while.

"Water first?" I ask, my voice a little better than yesterday, but still hoarse and raspy. The doctor said it could take weeks until my vocal chords are fully healed.

Ben puts down the ice cream and presses a button by my bed and a buzzing motor springs into life, lifting the top end of the mattress until I'm sitting up. I smile again at his thoughtfulness. He holds the glass to my lips, but I gently take it away from him. I'm stronger today, I can hold it myself. He frowns when he sees the cannula peeking out from a piece of tape on the back of my hand. A nurse removed the bag of fluids it had been connected to at some point in the early morning.

"Are you still in pain?" he asks, worry tinging his voice.

I just shrug and take another small sip of water. Drinking hurts but it also soothes my throat at the same time.

"Shall I ask the doctors to get you some painkillers?"

"It's okay," I whisper, trying not to strain my voice too much. "Better. Than. Yesterday."

"Don't talk." He smiles. "Eat your ice cream instead."

He hands me a paper cup with half molten chocolate goodness inside. There are even little chocolate pieces floating on top of the ice cream. It's just what I need.

I have to take small spoons as swallowing still hurts. I don't think ice cream has ever tasted this good. Ben watches me with amusement as I savour every spoonful with delight, but I don't mind. He brought me ice cream, he's okay.

After I've scraped the last morsels from the paper cup, I sink back, exhausted from all the movement. It's strange how I don't have any injuries on my body besides the bruised throat, my broken ankle and a few scratches on my arms, but still everything hurts. There's a fatigue to it all, a tiredness in every single one of my muscles. I'm slowly beginning to realise that it will take me some time to recover, not just because my ankle is in plaster. I think I'm malnourished as well, which isn't helping.

Even though I'm still confused about Ben's motives, the thought of having somewhere to stay that isn't a church or a cold bit of pavement does make my future look a little better.

"Do you want more?" he asks, pointing at my empty cup.

"No," I whisper. "Thank you."

"It's nothing. How are you feeling?"

"Been better." I attempt a brave smirk.

"The police are wanting a statement soon. I've told them to get some pen and paper so you don't have to talk." He hesitates for a moment. "Would you like me to stay when they come?"

"Yes, please." I don't know when Ben changed from the mysterious stalker to a person I trusted, but it feels good. Even though this trust is totally irrational. I still don't know the first thing about this man.

"Tell me about yourself," I croak, closing my eyes. I don't want to sleep, but it's hard keeping my eyelids from closing.

He stays quiet for a moment, before taking a deep breath. "I'm not sure what to tell you. My name is Ben, I'm thirty-one, I work for a government agency, and I like photography."

It sounds like something he's learned by heart. A biography, the soulless shell around the man.

"No, tell me about *you*," I repeat, putting the emphasis on the final word.

He doesn't reply and with each passing second, doubt bubbles up in me. Maybe I was wrong to trust him. If he's not letting me into his world, how am I supposed to give him access to mine?

Finally, he sighs. "I don't actually like photography.

It's just something I say because it makes me sound hip and creative. I like looking at photos, but I'm terrible at taking them. I would love to learn to paint though, one day. What I really like to do is archery. Not the modern kind they do at the Olympic Games. I have a longbow at home that I sometimes take into the woods to practice." He lowers his voice. "Don't tell anyone, it's not strictly speaking legal."

I smile. I can imagine him in the forest, bow slung over his shoulder; a modern version of Legolas. Hunting for prey, stalking it, keeping his brown eyes trained on it until he's in position.

"Hunt animals?" I whisper, my voice fading.

"Oh no, I just shoot at targets I put up. I grew up in a vegetarian hippie household, so I don't think I could ever kill an animal. It's not about shooting to kill, it's about the calm that comes before you release the string, the tension that suddenly gives way to total calm. Once the arrow is shot, you keep the bow in the same position for a breath or two, and that's the most relaxing feeling I can imagine. Knowing that you achieved something, and somehow released some of your own tension in the process." He sighs. "I don't have a lot of time for archery nowadays. Work always gets in the way. But maybe once my current... project is completed, I might have a chance to do it more regularly again."

He goes quiet again. I feel like I'm not going to hear much more from him today. He's not used to talking about himself, that much is clear. I'm amazed he already opened up this much.

A knock on the door ends our conversation, and a

bubble of anxiety grows in my chest as I realise that I will have to tell my story now, relive what happened last night.

"Is she awake?" a woman whispers.

"Yes, she's just exhausted," Ben replies and I can hear them move towards the bed. "Emily, are you up for this?"

I force my eyes to open. Better get this over with.

"Yes. Painkillers?" It's strange how my sentences have been reduced to single words. With speaking being so painful, I'm being selective about what to say. It's frustrating; usually I can't shut up. Now I'm forced to let others do all the talking.

"I'll get you something, be back in a moment," Ben says and exits the room, leaving me alone with two female police officers. One of them hands me a notepad and a pencil. I grip it tightly, not wanting it to slip from my weak hands.

"We're going to keep this as short as possible, okay?" the younger officer says and takes a seat on the chair where Ben was sitting just a moment ago. Her colleague stays standing, watching me with a mixture of empathy and curiosity.

"For the records, could you please write down your full name and date of birth."

By the time I'm done, trying to make my shaking hand write it halfway legible, Ben returns with a nurse. While she is giving me some intravenous pain meds, Ben sits down on my bed. "Just tell us when it gets too much, okay?"

When the nurse has left, he nods at the police officers to continue. It's a bit odd, they are looking at him like

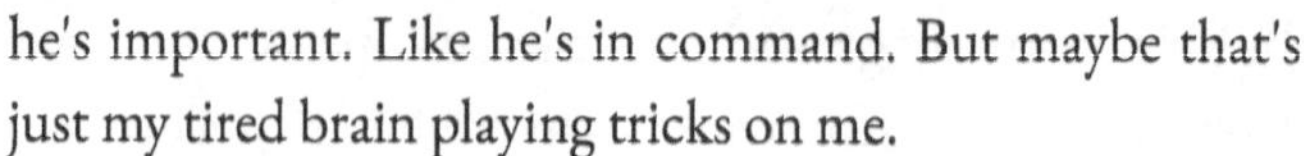

he's important. Like he's in command. But maybe that's just my tired brain playing tricks on me.

"How long have you been without a permanent residence?"

*21st September*, I write. I'm not going to forget that day anytime soon. Our relationship had been troubled for a while, but the way she told me to move out was harsh even for her. I can't believe how I managed to stay with my ex for three years. I was close to leaving several times, but then she would be nice for a few days, treating me like a delicate flower, before falling into her old patterns again. The patterns that sometimes left bruises on my skin. She made me believe it was all my fault. That she didn't have another choice than to get angry. That it was me who made her explode in fits of rage.

The weeks I lived on the streets were better than therapy. I realise now that our relationship was abusive and that it should never have gone on as long as it did.

"Where were you going last night? Can you write down a quick summary of what you did yesterday?"

I do as she asks, trying to remember where I went. It's all a bit foggy; the only thing that is very clear in my mind is the moment Ben saw me on the Royal Mile. The shame of him seeing me like this. The anger at how he seemed to be stalking me.

"Did you meet the suspect where you were found or did you walk there together?"

I frown at her calling the man a *suspect*. Clearly he's the attacker; he was arrested while trying to strangle me.

*He wanted money. I didn't have any, but he became*

*pushy and when I tried to get away from him, I fell and injured my ankle. I was lying on the ground and he*

I can't continue writing, I'm shaking too much. My hands are trembling and I notice my breathing becoming quicker.

"It's okay, Em, you're safe now," Ben whispers soothingly and gently takes my hand, squeezing it reassuringly. "I know it's hard, but we want this bastard to be locked up, so we need your statement. Is it okay if I ask you a few yes and no questions? That way you don't have to write."

"That's not advisable, sir. Closed questions may influence her statement," the older police officer interjects.

Did she really call Ben 'sir'? I look at him questioningly and he whispers, "I'll explain later."

He turns to the woman. "It's either that or you'll have to come back another time."

She sighs. "Go ahead."

Ben squeezes my hand again and I look at him, my anxiety slowly lessening. I can do this.

"Did you know this man?" I shake my head, then notice that it hurts too, so instead, I draw write 'no' on the paper.

"Had you ever seen him before?" Another 'no'.

The first ten questions or so he asks me are easy. But I know it won't stay that way. I'm getting tired; the pain meds are finally kicking in.

"Before he put his hands around your throat, did he touch you somewhere else?" I draw a tick and his grip on my hand tightens. A muscle twitches on his right cheek, almost unnoticeable, but he is all I'm looking at. Focussing on him helps me stay in the present.

"Can you show me where?" I move my other hand to my breast, trembling as I remember *his* touch there.

"Did you struggle?"

I draw another tick. "I almost got free," I whisper, a stray tear running down my face. Ben gently wipes it away. "Ankle," I add as an explanation for why I didn't run.

"Was that why he tried to strangle you?" Yes.

"This may be a strange question, but do you think he wanted to kill you rather than just make you unconscious?"

Shivering, I think back to what the man said when he put his bony fingers around my throat. Then I nod. Yes, he said I didn't need to be alive.

Ben turns to the two women. "Is that enough?"

"Yes, although we'll need to get a full statement once she can talk again."

Letting go of my hand, Ben gets up and accompanies the officers out of the room, talking to them outside. Without his support, the memories come crashing over me again. I'm shaking and I can't stop imagining those pale hands roaming my body. The fingers around my neck, squeezing tight. The pain. The fear. No air. I'm gasping, trying to get him off, make him let me go. His hands are everywhere, touching me, defiling me. I whimper in between gasping breaths. It hurts so much.

"Shit!" Hands grip my shoulders. "Em, listen to me. You're safe, it isn't real. Breathe, Em, breathe!"

There are sirens again as everything repeats itself. The

black spots in front of my eyes. The pressure on my chest. The voices. And then the silent, dreamless sleep.

# Six

en's house is massive. No, not *his*, he said it belonged to one of his flatmates. He also said that they would be waiting for us. Waiting to meet *me*. Apparently, they didn't have a problem at all with a random woman coming to live with them. Maybe they're used to Ben taking in strays.

He helps me out of the car, handing me my crutches. He's also got a wheelchair in the boot of his car because I'm still too weak to hop on crutches for too long, but it's only a short way through an iron-wrought gate to the main door. There's a brass lion knocker grimacing at me. Not the friendliest sight. Ben steps around me to unlock the door and leads me into a spacious living room. A giant red couch with matching footrests is taking up almost an entire wall, with bookshelves lining two of the others. I take to this place immediately. I limp to the sofa and fall back into its softness. After lying in bed for three days, sitting in the car and walking into the house has made me exhausted. Ben slides a footrest closer and helps me put my leg up. He's so... caring. My ex would have never done anything like this, and he's not even my partner. He's just a random guy who seems to like being friendly and helpful. Who has offered me a job he won't tell me anything about. And two flatmates who I don't know anything about either. This whole thing is one giant mystery. And I'm not sure if I like that.

"I'll get the others," he announces. "Do you want anything to drink?"

"Tea," I croak and he smiles.

"No hot chocolate?"

My eyes widen. Did he say the magic words?

"Oh yes," I sigh, already tasting the chocolate in my mouth. With a chuckle, he leaves. I look around the room. There's a sort of rolled up fabric on top of the bookshelf opposite - and a projector just above me. Instead of a tv they seem to have a little home cinema. Wow.

I can't make out what kind of books these guys are reading, but on a little tray table to my left a book called "Bad Science" awaits its next reader. It's well-worn and slightly bent at the edges. One of the men must really love it. I'm not one for non-fiction though, I prefer novels; stories I can lose myself in. Books have been my escape for as long as I can remember. And now I'm in a room with hundreds of them.

Two long, thin speakers hang from the ceiling to both sides of the bookshelf opposite, but that's the only technology besides the projector. No laptops, phones, tablets lying around like they did at my old flat. But what do I know? Maybe they're keeping their tech in their bedrooms.

I'm still having trouble imagining three grown men living together. Isn't that a little too much testosterone in one place?

There's a knock against the doorframe and in come two men who couldn't be any different from each other. The first one is pale and, with his white-blond hair, he could almost be an albino. He is tall and lithe, his black suit hugging his frame. His bright blue eyes pierce through me even from the distance. The guy behind him is just as tall, but also twice as broad - not fat, just very, very muscly. His ebony skin is in stark contrast to the white apron wrapped across his front. Long brown dreadlocks are falling down his shoulders, disappearing over his back. I will him to turn around so I can see how long they are. He's smiling widely, while the first guy is looking rather serious.

"Boys, get out of the way."

Ben presses past them, carefully balancing a giant mug filled to the brink with steaming cocoa. I gratefully take it from him, my fingers brushing over his scarred skin by accident. Once I can talk properly again, I will ask him about those scars.

"Em, meet Alistair, the laird of this home," he points to the blond guy, "and Luther, our cook." Luther punches him playfully in the ribs and Ben cries out in mock pain, before adding, "And friend. And colleague. Better?"

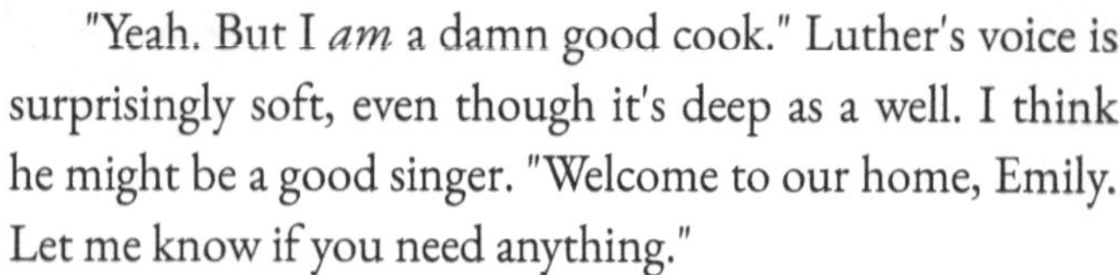

"Yeah. But I *am* a damn good cook." Luther's voice is surprisingly soft, even though it's deep as a well. I think he might be a good singer. "Welcome to our home, Emily. Let me know if you need anything."

"Thanks," I whisper, but Ben puts a finger on his lips.

"No talking. The less you talk, the quicker your voice will heal. We're going to stick to yes and no questions." He glances at the collar I'm still having to wear for the next few days. "But be careful with your nodding. Maybe we should agree on some hand gestures."

"Oh leave her alone, Ben," Alistair complains. "She's injured, not an invalid."

And with that, he leaves the room, not saying a single thing to me. I look at Ben, confused and a little hurt.

"He's having a bad day," Ben explains. "He's usually a little more... welcoming."

"Which is why I'm making him lasagne," Luther says cheerfully. "He always perks up after that. I hope you're not a vegetarian?"

I shake my head and wince at the pain shooting through my neck.

Ben clucks his tongue. "Hand gestures it is. One finger for no, the whole hand for yes. Wiggling fingers for maybe."

I put up one finger and Luther laughs while Ben looks a little shocked at me showing him *that* finger. Just because I can't speak doesn't mean that I have to be meek.

"I'll leave you two alone, I don't want our dinner to burn." Luther gives me a final grin before he leaves, closing the door behind him.

"Do you want to stay here for now or shall I show you your studio?" Ben asks, before shaking his head. "Sorry, I didn't think. One question at a time. Do you want to stay here?"

I put up my hand, smiling sheepishly. This is weird, but I have to admit, it's better than nodding.

"Dinner shouldn't be long. Shall we watch tv?"

I show him one finger - the index one this time. I've been without a telly for weeks and I'm not really missing it. I've occasionally followed the news by getting a free Metro newspaper at the train station, but my life has been exciting enough without having to watch others have adventures.

"Mmhm, we could annoy Alistair by messing with the order of the books. He likes to have them all sorted by title while I prefer to sort by author. Luther says that one day, he'll sort them by colour just so we stop bickering." He pauses, shrugging a little embarrassed. "Sorry, I'm rambling. I'm not used to having such one-sided conversations. Especially not after how you were when we first met. Although I wouldn't call that a conversation... more like an argument?"

I wiggle my fingers. He's got a point. I wasn't very nice to him.

I point at the speakers hanging from the ceiling. I've not listened to music in a long time.

"Okay, music it is." He walks to the bookshelf to our right and does something I can't see, but a second later Adele's *Hello* sounds from all around me. I lift an eyebrow and he shrugs.

"It's usually Alistair who uses the sound system, must be what he last listened to."

I can't tell if he's lying or not. But then, who cares if one of the guys likes Adele? It's good music.

Ben hands me a tiny remote, smaller than a bank card and almost as thin. "Feel free to change it to something you like. I don't know much about music."

I stare at him. How can you not have a taste in music? Music is everywhere. And it's beautiful.

Ben sits down on the sofa, leaving a small distance between us for which I'm grateful. I'm beginning to get comfortable around him, but I still don't entirely trust him. A tiny voice in my head is telling me to leave, to run, but it must have forgotten that my ankle is in plaster and my body is too weak to do much moving.

We sit together, listening to Adele, each lost in their own thoughts.

♥

Having emptied my plate, I give Luther the thumbs up. His lasagne truly was amazing. The guys finished ages ago and have been watching me eat tiny bite by tiny bite. My throat is better, well enough to eat solid food again, but I'm still taking it slowly.

Luther grins as he takes away our plates. "Ready for dessert?"

My hand shoots in the air, both to say yes and to show how ready I am. I'm full, but I had a sneak peek at the sticky toffee pudding he was putting in the oven when he pulled out the lasagne, and it looked ridiculously amazing. I don't know what Luther does for a living, but I wouldn't be surprised if he really was a cook.

Ben gets up to make us some tea (for Alistair and me) and coffee (for Luther and him), which leaves me alone with Alistair. He's looking a little friendlier now that he's eaten, and he even smiled once during dinner when Luther made a joke. Now he's watching me in the same way I'm watching him. He's even harder to read than Ben. I don't know if he wants me here, tolerates me or wants me to leave. It's his house, so I assume Ben had to ask him before he brought me here.

His pale eyes are mesmerising, despite the frown just above them. He's pretty; no, he's hot. Not in the usual masculine hotness-way, but he has his own, delicate beauty. I'm wondering whether it's impolite to ask if he's an albino. Is that offensive? But then I remember that I'm not allowed to talk, so for now that question is moot.

We continue to stare at each other, and I'm trying hard to match his poker-face. This is turning into something of a contest. I blink, and he does the same. Curious. I try not to blink and keep my eyes open. When my eyelids begin to flutter, I fight the urge until my eyes get teary. He's not blinking either, but a slight curve to his lips is slowly appearing. Is he trying to hide a smile? Then he blinks and with a sigh, I can finally do the same. Pointedly looking at his lips, I raise an eyebrow. He raises his. What the fuck. The guy is toying with me, mirroring my every move. I'm going to show him. I wiggle my ears - and now he's stuck. Not many people can do that.

He laughs and breaks our eye contact.

"Welcome to my home," he chuckles, reaching out to

shake my hand. I take it and he grips it tightly. I press as hard as I can. I can play this game, too. He is stronger though and is almost crushing my fingers. I open my mouth to complain, but he immediately lets go and puts a finger on his lips, just like Ben did earlier.

"Don't forget the rules. No talking. And while we're at it, you should know the other rules in the Cottage. Some rooms are locked, they are out of bounds. Do not try to find a key. Don't go into the basement. Don't go into the attic either. My bathroom is my bathroom, no one else gets to use it."

"That's because he's got a jacuzzi," Luther interrupts us, carrying a large glass dish using purple oven gloves. Purple, seriously?

He puts the steaming pudding in front of me so I can admire its sugary goodness. If the smell is anything to go by, this will be the best sticky toffee pudding I've ever eaten.

Ben joins us, handing out small bowls already filled with vanilla ice cream. These men really like to eat. I'm happy to follow their lead. For the past few weeks, I've lived off sandwiches and whatever Tesco had in their reduced section. This is a million times better.

While I'm taking the first bite - it's heavenly - Alistair continues with his rules.

"No running around. No parties. No loud music when I'm working. Don't touch my car."

"Are you quite finished?" Ben asks with a mixture of amusement and annoyance. "I can't remember you ever telling us half of these rules."

"This is different," Alistair grumbles. "We've not had a girl in this house before."

I wish I could talk. I'd have quite a few things to say to him, most of them not very polite. It's probably good that I can't. I don't want to offend my host. Yet.

"I'm sure Emily will be no different from either of us. And besides, she's got her own space in the studio, she might not spend as much time here anyways."

Luther winks at me. "But you're welcome to stay in this part of the house as much as you like."

I grin at him. He reminds me of a friend I used to have as a child. Granted, he was imaginary and a bear, but he was just as friendly and cuddly. Not that I think Luther is cuddly. It's just that with all his bulk, he could be comfortable to lean against.

Alistair pulls out his phone. "What size are you?"

I stare at him. That's not something a guy asks me very often.

He sighs in exasperation. "You need clothes."

I hold up both hands, wiggling all ten fingers.

"Size ten? I would have guessed eight."

I don't tell him that I prefer to wear baggy clothes. I don't really want him to get me clothes in the first place. I hate being indebted to people.

He types on his phone while the rest of us devour our pudding. I'm the slowest again; my throat is beginning to hurt and so is my ankle. Once we're done with dinner, I really need to put it up again.

"Want me to show you your new home?" Ben asks as I put the spoon in my bowl with a plonk. I put up my hand

and he grins. "We're making progress. Good. Can you walk or shall I carry you?"

With an indignant look in his direction, I get up, jumping on one leg to the wall that I leant my crutches against. Everything hurts, but I'm not giving him the satisfaction of seeing it.

"See you later," Luther calls as I follow Ben out into the corridor.

# Seven

There's a brand-new phone lying on my pillow. When he notices my confusion, Ben explains, "Alistair thought you might need it. It will make communication easier. He's added all our numbers."

I can't help it, I turn around and hug Ben. The crutches are probably hurting him, but he's hugging me back, gently holding me in his strong arms. He smells of cinnamon and something else, something that makes me want to lick his skin to find out. His hands are drawing lazy circles on my back. Only now do I notice how much I've craved human touch. Nobody has touched me in the past few weeks, at least nothing more than a handshake or an accidental brush against my skin when someone was putting money into my bowl. Now that I'm in Ben's arms, I don't want it to end.

When we break apart, I want to cry as the feeling of loneliness returns, but I keep up my poker face and don't show my feelings when Ben asks whether I need anything and then leaves. I sit on the bed, not quite knowing what to do. It's been a while since I've had my own flat. This place isn't big; it's basically one large room separated into a sleeping and an eating area with a tiny kitchenette and a small table. A bookcase is strategically placed in the middle of the room, forming a partition that makes the studio feel larger. A small bathroom completes my new home. I decide to skip having a shower tonight as I'm not quite sure how to do it without getting my plaster wet. At the hospital, a nurse helped me, and I had a little plastic chair to sit down on in the shower. Here, I have neither. And I'm not planning to ask any of the guys for help.

Next to the phone, Alistair has left a large t-shirt for me; judging from the size it may be Luther's. It will do for sleeping in, it's better than sleeping in my clothes again. The room is nice and warm, so I don't worry about it being not enough. On top of the shirt is a toothbrush and a pack of travel toiletries, the kind you get on a long-haul flight. I'm touched by the thoughtfulness. Alistair seemed so hostile in the beginning, but now that I see how he prepared my room for my arrival, I'm rethinking that first impression. Maybe there's more to him that meets the eye.

I yawn and decide it's time for bed. Tomorrow I'm going to ask the guys about the mysterious job, and why they want me here. I'm still suspicious. Now that I'm thinking about it, I get up and limp to the door, locking it. I may have started to trust Ben, but I don't know the other two.

Before I switch off the light, I check my new phone. It's smooth in my hand, I assume it must have been expensive. Strange. Who buys a random person a phone, and one so expensive at that?

There's a new message from someone called Superman.

Superman: *Sleep well. Call if you need anything. Ben.*

I smile and am about to put away the phone when a new message arrives with a ding.

Gladiator: *Sweet dreams.*

Guess that's Luther. I don't think Alistair would call himself Gladiator. No message from him. I check the phone book though. The only other person in there is called Genius. That's not pretentious at all.

I send Superman and Gladiator a quick "good night" and switch off the phone. Time to sleep.

♥

Hands are pulling me under the water's surface, their nails burying themselves deep into my calves. I'm gasping for air, but all that enters my lungs is water. It tastes brackish, like dead bodies have been decomposing in it. I try to see who's attacking me, but the water is too murky and hurts my eyes. All I feel are the hands on my body, pulling me down, hurting me. I kick, hitting something, but it's no use, someone else takes their place immediately, adding their clawed grip to that of the others. My arms are fighting to keep me above the surface, but there are too many. I'm drowning; no, I'm being drowned.

I open my mouth and scream into the water, bubbles floating to the surface which is drifting further and further away. Maybe someone will see them. The last sign that I was alive, that I was here. My movements are getting sluggish with exhaustion and lack of oxygen. Something bites my leg and rips out a chunk of my flesh. I know I'm dying and it feels familiar. I'm returning to a place I've been before, and I remember now that it wasn't all that bad. It's like coming home. I stop screaming and no longer fight. Giving in is both a terrible and beautiful thing to do. I whimper as the final wave swallows me and I'm pulled into the depths of the murky waters.

Suddenly, something is embracing me, breathing oxygen into my lungs. I return the hug, wrapping myself around them. The bites have stopped and only pain remains in my leg. The bad people have gone.

I relax and let go.

♥

"Hot chocolate or tea?"

Those must be the best words in the world to wake up to.

"Both?" I mumble, snuggling against the thing that just spoke to me. The *thing*. The human. The man. Ben.

He's in my bed.

Suddenly wide awake, I open my eyes and sit up, clutching the duvet to my chest.

"What...?" My voice stops working after the first word. I forgot about that. Ben is lying opposite me, smiling. His hair is ruffled and a trace of a beard has appeared on his face overnight.

"Shhh, no talking. You had a nightmare and when I

came to see if everything was alright, you kind of pulled me into the bed and wrapped yourself around me."

Oh, I didn't expect him to say that. I'm trying to remember any dreams I may have had, but my mind is empty.

"How... door?" I ask, ignoring his stern glance.

He grins sheepishly. "You were screaming, so I... kind of... broke in."

I glance at the door which looks a little worse for wear. Wood splinters are covering its side and I'm sure it was a little straighter when I closed it last night. He must have used a lot of force to get in.

"Out," I whisper, trying to make my voice stern and uncompromising. Unfortunately, he follows my command, taking the duvet with him.

At my protesting grumble, he smiles innocently.

"You said out, so I thought you wanted the blanket out, too. Better get dressed or you'll get cold."

And with that, he leaves, closing the broken door behind him with a loud creak. How the hell did I not hear that? And why would I ever snuggle against him like that? I don't know the guy. I've had a terrible experience only a few days ago. You'd think I'd stay away from physical contact for a while, especially with men. Instead, I used him like a teddy bear.

I get dressed in my old, dirty clothes, which takes a while thanks to a plastered foot that refuses to fit easily through the trouser leg. After a lot of prodding, I'm finally ready to begin the day.

. . .

Luther and Ben are waiting in the kitchen, and so are two mugs on the table. I raise an eyebrow.

"You said you wanted both," Ben shrugs and Luther chuckles as he sees my indecision at what to drink first.

"What do you want for breakfast? We've got cereal and toast, but I could also make you some eggs or pancakes," Luther says, an empty bowl in front of him. I don't want to make too much of a fuss, so I go with cornflakes and a banana from the fruit basket in the centre of the large kitchen table.

My throat is still sore, but eating is getting better with every meal. Hopefully I'll be able to speak again soon.

Once the hot chocolate is comfortably settled inside my stomach, I take the mug of tea between my hands and look at the guys expectantly.

"What does she want?" Luther asks Ben, who shrugs.

"No idea."

I sigh in frustration. Isn't it obvious? I pull out my phone and signal them to do the same.

Em: *What is the job? Why am I here?*

"You still haven't told her?" Luther asks.

"I've not had a chance yet. And I was planning to do it with you two there."

Luther shrugs. "Well, Alistair is out for the day, so we either have to wait until tonight or we do it now without him."

I type quickly before they continue their conversation without me.

Em: *Now.*

Ben sighs. "Let's go into the living room. I'll take your mug, Emily."

Again, I'm surprised by his awareness. Most people wouldn't have noticed that with my crutches, carrying a drink would be impossible.

I follow the two men into the living room, taking the same seat on the sofa as yesterday. Again, Ben helps me put my leg up. I could get used to this. I don't think anybody has ever been this caring.

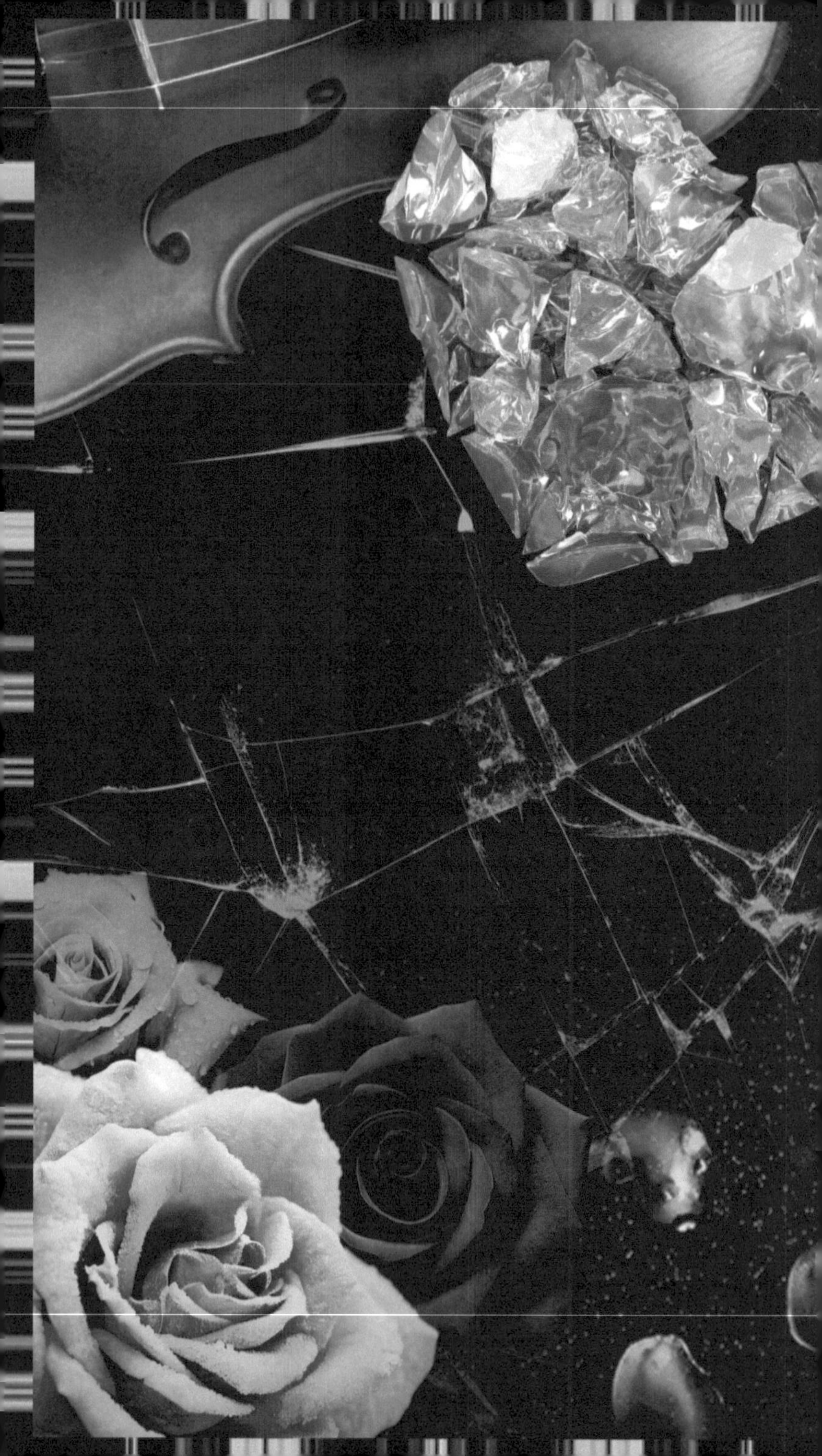

# Eight

Luther rummages through a folder he's taken from the bookshelf. "We need you to sign an NDA first. This is not something to leave this room, okay?"

He hands me a pen and a stack of papers, neatly stapled together at the top.

"Take your time reading through this. I know I'm probably the only person who ever reads the small print in contracts, but I want you to know exactly what you're signing."

Ben huffs impatiently. "All it's saying is that this is a secret, that you will have to keep the secret whether you take the job or not. If you take it, you will have to sign a more extensive agreement."

Enjoying his impatience, I carefully read through the contract. In the end, it turns out to be exactly what Ben said. It doesn't even mention anyone besides the three guys. Here I was hoping to find out more about who they're working for.

I sign it and hand it back to Luther, who checks my signature and puts it back into the folder. I wonder how many other people's contracts are in there.

"Do you want to explain or shall I?" he asks Ben, who sighs again, as if this is all one big chore.

"You do it, you're better at this kind of stuff."

Luther takes a seat on the sofa between me and Ben. I notice how he's careful to leave enough space between us that he doesn't touch me.

"I don't know how much Ben has mentioned, but if I know him at all, it won't have been much."

Ben opens his mouth to protest, but Luther doesn't let him interrupt.

"Alistair, Ben and I work in intelligence. We're part of a government agency, operating under the command of the Serious Organised Crime Agency, or SOCA. We're specialising in gang crime in Edinburgh, but because of the nature of it, sometimes we're working all over Scotland and the UK."

I type on my phone.

Em: *You're police?*

"Not quite," Ben says, seemingly annoyed that Luther didn't manage to get the point across. "Think more like secret service."

Em: *Spies?*

"We don't like that word," Luther chuckles. "It's too negative."

"Yeah, we prefer Scottish James Bond," Ben adds with a smirk. "Except that our codenames aren't 007, 008 and 009."

Em: *What are they?*

"Later. You wanted to know about your job?" Luther asks and I nod. "As part of our current investigation, we're needing help with translation. It's sensitive material so we can't go through a normal translation agency. We also don't want to have to employ three different people to cover Italian, Albanian and Russian. There's a reason why our team is small."

Em: *Brain, muscles, Ben?*

Luther laughs while Ben looks annoyed. "I will let you know that I am the leader of this team. So be careful what you say."

He winks, totally destroying the effect of his previous statement.

"On paper, yes, but in real life, I'm the leader," Luther stage-whispers.

Em: *I still don't get why you'd go through so much trouble to employ a translator.*

"We don't just need someone sitting in an office, doing the translations for us," Ben explains. "We need someone who can come with us as an interpreter, someone who's smart and can look after herself."

I huff, point at my collar and type on my phone.

Em: *Do I seem like I can look after myself?*

Ben sighs and looks at me, his eyes serious. "You've taken self-defence and kickboxing classes. You've had a rough upbringing and still managed to get a first-class degree at university. You speak four languages fluently. And you managed to live on the streets for several weeks in the midst of winter. So yes, I think you can look after yourself."

I wordlessly point to my leg and Luther takes my hand, squeezing it reassuringly.

"Anyone could have ended up in that situation, Emily. You were unprepared, you got injured, you had no choice to defend yourself. Hell, they say you managed to hit him several times. You fought, and that's what counts. And you're not cowering in a corner right now, you're here, ready to create a new future for yourself. I'd say we'd be lucky to have you on board."

I don't know what to say, even if I could speak. Luther doesn't know me, and yet he knew exactly what to say. He made me feel better with just a few words. He's mentioned the attack, yet I'm not scared again.

Ben clears his throat. "At the beginning, when I found out you were living rough, I thought that might be an added bonus. The homeless community is a great asset in finding out information. They're not noticed and, when they are, they're usually ignored, but they see a lot. Having a contact on the streets seemed... beneficial. And you looked innocent enough, someone who's not used to it, who would talk to people who've been homeless for a while, trying to get their advice. And who, in the process, might talk to some of the gangs we're investigating."

There it is. They want me to live on the streets again. This is not about me getting a new life. They want me to stay in my old one, help them with their *intelligence*, whatever that means, while still being in the same fucking situation. No, I'm not going to do this. At the hospital they offered to get in touch with social services to get me some temporary accommodation while my leg healed. I should have just accepted that and not followed Ben into the unknown.

I get up, almost falling onto Luther's lap while trying to find my balance, and limp to the corner where my crutches are parked.

"What are you doing?" Ben asks. "Do you need the toilet?"

I'd love to tell him exactly what I'd like to do with his head and the toilet, but I don't want to waste any words on him. I walk out of the room towards the studio. This was all a dream. I should have seen it coming.


When I've finally made it through the long hallway and into my little flat, I lean against the door, closing my eyes. I'm not going back on the streets. With my leg, I'll be an easy target for any pervert wanting to stick his dick somewhere.

"Everything okay?" a soft voice asks and I jump, forgetting about my ankle, stumbling, falling - into Alistair's arms. "Woah, easy, girl. I didn't think I was that scary."

He helps me up, but I step back, bringing some distance between us. Maybe this is why Alistair was so cold from the start. He didn't want to form any attachments to someone they'd send away again soon. Now, I better do the same.

"I was just bringing you the clothes I got," he explains, but I interrupt him.

"I'm leaving," I whisper hoarsely, walking to the wardrobe where I put my coat.

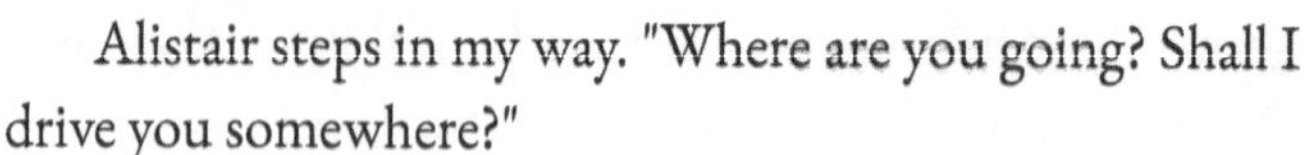

Alistair steps in my way. "Where are you going? Shall I drive you somewhere?"

Why is he suddenly so friendly? This is making it harder.

I shake my head, cursing the collar still stabilising my neck. I undo the velcro at the back and pull it off, exposing my skin to fresh air again. It feels good.

"What are you doing? What's wrong?

"Leaving," I say again, slipping into my coat while balancing on one leg.

"But you've got nowhere to go. Didn't those two idiots explain? Even if you don't take the job, you can stay until we can find you an alternative." He runs a hand through his white blonde hair, clearly not sure what to do.

His words almost make me pause, but no, I will not be thrown out again. I will leave on my own terms this time. Maybe if I go back to the hospital, they can talk to the housing people like they said they would before I was discharged. It's not even noon yet, so I have a few hours to find somewhere to stay the night.

I look around the room. There are no other possessions here that I can take with me. It was a dream, nothing more.

I turn to leave, but Alistair is blocking the door, arms crossed in front of his chest.

"I'm not letting you run away just like that before you tell me why. It's not safe. Let me get the others and we can have a chat, okay?"

I shake my head and immediately regret it as my neck

muscles protest. Alistair notices my sharp intake of breath and looks at me with worry in his eyes.

"You were only released from hospital yesterday and they said that you need to give yourself time to heal. Don't make any rash decisions now. Let's talk about this. Give us a chance to help you."

I blink away the tears threatening to come into the open.

"I. Don't need. Help," I try to say, hoping he'll understand my hoarse voice. "Won't. Be Used."

His eyes widen. "Nobody is planning to use you. Why would you think that?"

I groan in frustration. I can't explain, and I don't want to. Just let me go.

I try to push past him, but me and my crutches are no match against Alistair. He stands his ground, not letting me squeeze past.

"Fuck you," I curse, surprised at how well my voice is working just now.

Instead of answering, he takes out his phone and presses a button on the side.

"Emergency button," he explains with a grin. "They'll come running any second now."

And true to his word, I can already hear doors slamming in the distance. Moments later, footsteps racing along the corridor, followed by knocking on the door.

"Al, what's going on?" Luther shouts from the hallway.

"Is Emily alright?" Ben sounds just as frantic.

Alistair shoots me a conspiratorial smile before

answering loudly. "You two upset our guest. What the fuck did you do?"

Silence follows. Then Ben, sounding totally confused, responds, "We gave her the contract. And told her about her job."

Alistair looks at me. "Is that right?"

I nod.

"But that's not what made you upset?"

I shake my head, ignoring the pain running down my spine.

"Lou, what did Ben say?" Alistair shouts. He could just open the door to make communication easier, but it looks like he's enjoying himself.

"Just what we'd discussed... And he told her that he thought she was clever and resourceful, and that she would... oh... damn."

"What was it?" Ben growls rather impatiently. It would be funny if it ... well, wasn't.

"You told her that she would be a great asset living on the streets. Right after you got her away from there. So now she probably thinks you're going to send her back. Make her sleep rough again."

"True?" Alistair whispers to me and I hold up a hand. "Is it okay if they come in? I think it's time to talk about this properly. No running away. No misunderstandings. If you still want to leave afterwards, I won't stop you."

I think for a moment, then hold up my hand again. What do I have to lose?

"Guys, you can come in now. But be nice!"

He steps back and leads me to the bed where we sit down together while the other two enter the room, looking sheepish. Ben takes a chair and places it in front of me until he can look straight into my eyes.

"I'm sorry, I didn't mean it like that." I raise an eyebrow, challenging him to continue. "I didn't mean that we'd send you back, make you homeless again. I told you at the beginning that you could stay with us, and that is still true. What I was talking about was what we intended before I met you. Before I could put a face, a personality to the woman I had read about in your file. I didn't think you'd be so innocent" - I laugh mirthlessly at that - "and after what happened, I would never, ever let you live like that again."

I signal to Alistair to hand me his phone, and I open a message to type.

Em: *It's not your choice.*

I pass the phone to Ben and he reads it out loud. He sighs. "True, it's not my choice where you live. But right now, I can offer you a safe place to stay. If you don't want the job, then you can stay nonetheless, no strings attached. I don't want you to live out there. Not you, not anyone."

Em: *That's not what it sounded like earlier.*

"That was Business-Ben speaking. Me, the real Ben, wouldn't want to send someone to sleep on the streets, unprotected, just to get some information we could likely get in other ways. It was just one of many options, one that we discarded. You don't need to fear us throwing you out. That won't happen. Promise."

Alistair grins. "In the end, it's my decision anyway, it's my house. And I'm hereby giving you this flat rent-free until you no longer want or need it. Nobody is using

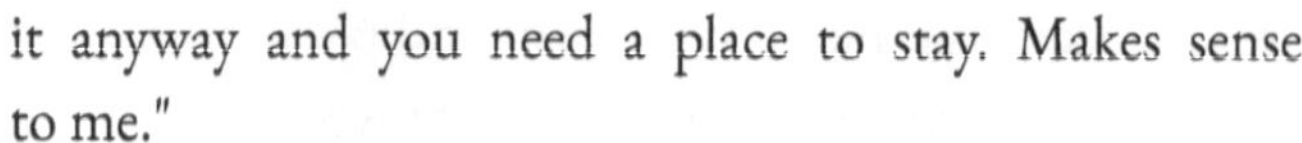

it anyway and you need a place to stay. Makes sense to me."

"Why?" I whisper. How am I supposed to believe that a random stranger would give me a room, for nothing in return? People just don't do that. There's always a row of strings attached, even if it's not obvious at first glance. Humans are not a selfless species.

"Ben, do you want to tell her?"

"No. You do it. I'm going to make us some tea." He gets up and leaves the room without a further word of explanation.

"He doesn't like to talk about it," Alistair explains. "His sister died four years ago from a drug overdose. She was sleeping rough in Glasgow and we think she may have been prostituting herself. They only found her two days after she died. Ben hadn't heard from her in weeks and didn't even know how bad she had it. He's been blaming himself ever since." He sighs. "So that's why he would never make you leave without any plans of where you were going to go. As I said, you can stay for as long as you want. And if you want to work with us, there's even a pay package included, so you could move to your own place, if you wanted."

Luther leans over and whispers, "It's a pretty good salary."

"That it is." Ben chooses this moment to return with a tray of four steaming mugs. One of them has a little hat of cream on top. He's made hot chocolate again. I could cuddle him for that. And for losing his sister that way. No wonder he was so persistent the first time we met.

I almost rip the mug away from him, licking the cream off - to the great amusement of the guys.

"No spoon," I mumble, using my tongue instead to remove more of the cream. First the cream, then the hot chocolate. I don't like it when it melts and then builds a film of fatty circles on top.

Ben holds up a spoon that must have been on the tray. "I could give you this, but it's much more fun watching you without one."

I stick out my tongue - still covered in cream - and he laughs, warming my heart just as much as the hot chocolate. He's a good guy.

Once I'm finished, we sit in comfortable silence. I ask Alistair to pass me his phone again.

Em: *I'm going to stay.*

# Nine

We have lunch together, but we don't talk much, preferring instead to focus on Luther's latest magical creation: salmon on a bed of spinach and pasta, sprinkled with olive oil and pine nuts.

Once I'm done, I take my phone and type a quick message.

Em: *Are you a cook, Luther?*

He chuckles. "No, but my dad was. I spent most of my weekends and school holidays helping out in the restaurant he worked at. He always wanted me to follow in his footsteps, but things turned out differently."

A shadow has fallen over his expression, but I don't ask what happened to derail his plans.

"We're lucky to have him," Ben says, still chewing after getting a second helping. "Otherwise we'd probably live off takeaways and frozen pizza. We'd be gigantic, even with our gym."

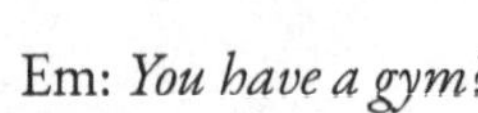

Em: *You have a gym?*

Luther nods. "Downstairs, I can show you later. Do you like going to the gym?"

Em: *I used to.*

Before Jess. Before she took away all of my hobbies and turned me into her pet, always catering to her whims. I never realised how much I lost during our relationship, but being away from her has made me see the truth. It hurts, but it's probably part of the healing process. As I said, living on the streets is better than therapy. It makes you realise all sorts of things.

"I can come up with some exercises for you where you don't put strain on your leg," Luther promises. "Once you're better. And if you want to brush up on your kickboxing, Al's the expert in that."

I shoot Alistair a surprised look. While his figure is definitely athletic, I didn't expect him to do martial arts for some reason. He seems too posh for that. Fencing, perhaps. Golf. God, I'm so full of bias and prejudice. Just because he's inherited a house and likes to wear expensive clothes doesn't mean he's grown up like that.

I lean back in my chair, a pleasant warmth radiating from my stomach. Being full is such a beautiful feeling. I'd got used to the knotted hunger pain in my belly while sleeping rough, but now I'm ready to forget how that felt. I want a normal life again, where I can eat until I'm full, sleep in a warm bed and not be afraid of everyone. These men seem to be offering me that but, while my heart wants to take it and hug them in gratitude, my brain won't stop sending me warning thoughts. I need to keep my guard up. They all seem really nice right now, but will that stay that way? Will they collect my debts at some point? Will translating be the only job they want me to do, or is there a more sinister reason they want me to stay in their house?

Luther puts a mug of hot chocolate in front of me and those thoughts get pushed away. I smile at him and reach for my phone again.

Em: *Are you fattening me up like a Christmas turkey?*

Luther laughs. "No, although you could do with a few more pounds around your hips. I just like watching you drink. I don't think I've ever seen anyone take so much pleasure in hot chocolate."

Em: *It's the drink of the Gods.*

Ben winks at me. "And the drink of the Goddess."

"Stop flirting," Alistair admonishes him with a grin. "I need to head out again, there are some gadgets I need to inspect."

Em: *Gadgets?*

"Think James Bond, only less sophisticated," Alistair explains, already on his way out. "There's a new guy who thinks he's a genius, and it's my task to show him that he's not." He grimaces and turns to the other two guys. "M wants a meeting afterwards, so I might be late, don't wait for me with dinner. If I'm lucky, we'll meet in her café and I'll get some cake."

He leaves before I can ask more questions. Ben gets up and starts to take out dishes, while Luther points at my mug.

"Drink up, I've got plans for what we can do this afternoon."

I drink my hot chocolate faster than its velvety smoothness deserves, but I'm too excited about what Luther meant. Are they going to tell me more about that mysterious job? The sooner I can start paying them back, the better. Alistair bought me several sets of clothes, all of them of better quality than I'd usually get for myself. He'd carefully taken off all the price tags, but I know that a small fortune is now hanging in my wardrobe. It makes me feel a little queasy. Jess always kept a tight grip on our money, so I mainly went to charity shops for new clothes. The trick in Edinburgh is to go to some of the richer parts of town, where the quality of clothes in charity shops is a lot better than in poorer areas like the one we lived in.

As soon as I'm done, Luther gets up and hands me my crutches. He leads me into the living room and points to the sofa, where I sit down at my usual place. Ben has followed us and puts the footstool in front of me so I can rest my leg. It's been hurting all day, but not as bad as it was at the beginning. I should probably ask for where Ben put the painkillers they gave me at the hospital, but that's for later.

"Please tell me you're not planning what I think you're planning," Ben groans when Luther heads to a cabinet in the corner. "Don't turn her into your new victim."

I look at him in confusion. That doesn't sound good in the slightest.

Luther laughs. "You just don't want to come last again."

He pulls out a large box from the cabinet and puts it

on the low table in front of me. Monopoly. He wants to play Monopoly.

I stare at him, then I laugh, and laugh, and laugh, tears streaming down my face, my throat hurting, my chest wheezing with the unfamiliar movement.

"What did I do?" Luther asks in confusion, and his concerned face makes me laugh even harder. Ben looks just as confused. My cheeks are flushed and my shirt is getting wet with tears, but I can't stop laughing.

"Tell us what's going on," Ben commands and hands me his phone. My hands are shaking, but my laughter is slowly ebbing away as I start to type.

Em: *It's so normal.*

He stares at me as if I'm completely crazy.

Em: *It's what friends do.*

Ben shows Luther the message and they both frown.

"Yes, maybe we want to be friends?" Luther says, his voice a little unsure. "Why is that funny?"

They're still not getting it. The laughter has finally stopped, but a grin is plastered across my face and I can't seem to make my mouth take on a different shape.

Em: *You. Me. Normal. Playing Monopoly. After all that's happened. It's too normal. Ordinary. Like we're normal people. Like we didn't all get hurt and broken.*

Another tear slides down my cheek, but this one isn't one born from laughter.

"Why do you say that?" Luther asks, his expression unreadable, dark. "What makes you think we got hurt?"

I look him straight in the eyes, then type.

Em: *Just because one of you carries his scars on the outside, doesn't mean that the rest of you don't have them. Unbroken people don't live in a house together with their colleagues. They have lives, families. They don't take in strays.*

I don't know where I get the confidence to write this. Why I feel like I *recognise* something within them that reminds me of myself. Maybe I'm being too forward. Maybe they'll throw me out now.

"You're not a stray," Ben says softly. "And you're right. We all have our broken parts, but we've helped each other mend them." He looks down at his scarred hand. "Mostly. Do you want to know how I got these?"

I'm suddenly not sure I want to. I shouldn't have laughed and brought this up. I should just have enjoyed playing a round of Monopoly.

Ben doesn't wait for an answer. "I got captured by the mafia organisation we were investigating two years ago. They didn't know I was working for SOCA, or they'd have probably killed me rather than torture me to find out who my employer was. An informant helped me escape, but not until they'd had some fun flaying my hand. Two of those responsible are now in prison, but a third is still at large. One day, we'll find him."

His eyes are fixed on his hand. The scars marring his skin suddenly seem even bigger, more intrusive. I want to reach out and hug him, but I don't. We're not at that stage of familiarity yet, and I'm not sure if we'll ever get there. I should keep my distance from these men. They might attract me because I can see the same vulnerability in them that I feel inside of me, but that might not be healthy. And maybe I'm mistaken about it all. I might be projecting my own pain onto them. Maybe they're not broken at all. Maybe I'm imagining it all. I've already established that I can't read them as well as I can read other people.

Luther clears his throat. "Monopoly?"

I wipe my face and give him a tense smile. Yes, let's play board games.

❤

We play all afternoon. Just like Ben predicted right at the start, Luther won all three rounds. We move on to Rummy and then, because Ben insisted, Bonanza. It's a card game about planting and trading funny looking beans and it's surprisingly fun. I win the first round and am tied with Luther in the second.

"I better make dinner," he announces when I demand a third round. He's just scared of losing to me again. "There's still some salmon left so I could make a salad."

"Salmon salad?" I croak before remembering that talking hurts.

"I think we'll need to start a talk jar for you," Ben announces. "Like a swear jar, except that you have to throw a coin in every time you try to talk."

Fuck. For a moment, I was happy and forgot all about my troubles, but now it's all back, racing around my mind. I sigh and take out my phone.

Em: *I don't have any money.*

Ben's expression darkens slightly and he gets up and walks to one of the bookshelves. From between two stacks of books, he takes a large jar. It's full of coins, not just pennies, one and two pound coins as well.

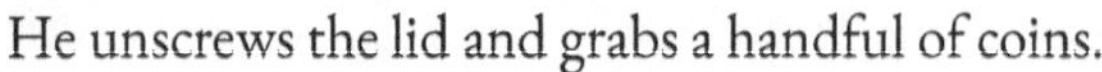

He unscrews the lid and grabs a handful of coins.

"Here you go. This is your budget. If you go over it, we'll have to come up with a... punishment."

His eyes flare with mirth at that last word and a shiver runs over my skin. Punishment sounds rather exciting when it's Ben talking about it.

I hesitate to accept the money, but as it's all for the talk jar and won't leave this house, I take it and put it in the pocket of the oversized hoodie I'm wearing. I didn't even notice Luther leaving, but he already returns with an empty beer glass.

"Didn't have anything better," he says with a chuckle. "You can put one in already."

I frown at him but throw in a pound coin. It's not like it's my money, so it's a lot less painful than a proper swear jar.

"I'll make dinner, you two do whatever you want," Luther announces and is gone before I can offer to help.

"Music?" Ben asks and I nod. Ouch. I need to get used to the hand gestures. How long until I can talk again? A few more days. It's going to feel like an eternity. I like to talk, a lot. This imposed vow of silence is making me annoyed.

He takes out the remote and presses a few buttons. This time, it's classical music rather than Adele. Someone must have been listening to it last night. Alistair, perhaps? It seems more likely than Luther, and Ben said he doesn't really listen to music. I wonder why he's doing it now, with me.

I settle onto the sofa and close my eyes, letting go of all my worries. I kind of wish Ben would put an arm around me but, for now, I enjoy being in the same room with someone who isn't a threat. Who doesn't shout. Who doesn't get violent. Just a normal, lovely person who seems to like me.

I smile at the thought. Yes, maybe we can become friends.

# Ten

There's a violin on the piano and it's calling to me.

I found this room just opposite of the living room and it's filled with instruments and bookshelves. There are drums in one corner, a guitar on a stand in another, and in the middle, the grand piano. I didn't expect there to be a music room in this house.

The guys are still in the kitchen, discussing the news we watched after dinner, so I dared to step closer and run my fingers over the polished wood. A violin. I haven't played one since... no. I step back and almost run into Alistair, who's staring at me curiously.

"Do you play?" he asks, a seductive melody swirling in his voice.

I shake my head and look down at the floor.

"Would you like to try?"

My heart gives a little jump. I'm given the chance to hold a violin again – but then my heart remembers and shudders. This will rip open too many old wounds. And

I've got enough to deal with as it is. Besides, I might not be able to play anymore; it's been years.

I hold up a finger to signal no, then point at Alistair as an encouragement for him to play.

He looks at me as if he's deciding what to do. Is he embarrassed to play in front of me?

He runs a finger over the polished wood, gently following the violin's curved body. He's so gentle, so tender, as if he's touching human skin.

"The violin was my mother's," Alistair says quietly. "We used to play together a lot."

"I'm sorry." I can't help but speak, but luckily, Alistair doesn't know about the talk jar yet. I hope.

"Oh no, she's not dead. It's just ... it's complicated."

Isn't everything. He's still staring at the violin with a wistful expression, then the muscles around his mouth tighten and he picks it up with one elegant motion, pressing its chinrest against his skin. He lifts the bow and before I can even admire the way his muscles flex, he begins to play.

It starts with a gentle, quivering sound, unsure and forlorn. Then the melody lifts, becoming stronger, more confident, although there's still a melancholy to it that makes me want to reach out and hug Alistair. His eyes are closed as he begins to play in earnest, his fingers pressing on the strings with more than just a mechanical intensity. He's *feeling* the music. The music is within him, and the bow and strings help him let it out from the prison of his soul. Lines of concentration appear on his forehead as he continues to play, faultlessly, not wavering once. This song must be embedded deep within his mind to play it with such precision. He handles the violin in a way others would a lover. I don't think anybody has ever touched me the way he embraces his instrument.

His fingers begin to dance along the strings, never meeting and yet working together to create the most beautiful melody. I don't know the song he's playing, but it somehow wriggles its way into my heart and touches things inside of there that I thought I'd forgotten.

My first violin lesson. The terrible sound the bow made on the strings. Me, devastated that it didn't sound like it was supposed to. The violin teacher, Mr Gabor, encouraging me to try again. Him putting my fingers in place, showing me how to make the violin sing. The bow, gently stroking the strings, enough to make a sound but not enough to make noise.

Sadness wells up in me. It all ended. That was the past. I had such high hopes then. Becoming a violinist. Playing to make my living. Turning my passion into a profession.

Of course, it didn't work out. Things never do. I've not touched a violin for years. I wonder if I could still do it. Coax the instrument to make beautiful music with me. Caress and seduce it while still being the one in charge. My fingers twitch, copying the movements of Alistair's hands on the fingerboard.

His eyes are closed, he's alone with the music and his violin. He's a master of this instrument, but I think he's one of the few people who realise that it's not him who creates the music. It's the violin. We just help make it audible.

By the time the song ends and Alistair opens his eyes

again, as if awakening from a dream, my cheeks are wet with tears.

He looks at me, his expression unreadable. I stare back into his beautiful pale eyes, wondering what's going on inside of him. He's a mystery, even more so than Ben. With Ben, I have the illusion of being able to read him. With Alistair, I have no hope of ever deciphering this man.

Not taking my eyes off his, I whisper, "That was beautiful."

He doesn't reply, just wordlessly offers me the violin.

My turn.

I hand him my crutches, leaning against the piano for support, and gingerly take the violin from him, unsure what to do. Should I play? Will it rip open old wounds? Should I let them?

The chin rest is warm. Alistair's warmth. Somehow, that gives me strength. He hesitated, yet he played. I will do the same.

I take the bow from his hands and lift it above the strings. I'm ready.

Alistair is still staring at me, his eyes piercing. I look away, unwilling to take the challenge.

I close my eyes and begin to play.

Until the bow touched the strings, I wasn't sure what I was going to play, but now, the music flows through me and I recognise the song. Pachelbel's canon, one of my favourites.

I smile, thanking my subconscious for making that choice, and let go, diving into the music. It's like I never stopped. My fingers know exactly what to do. My shoulders feel a little achy, not having been in this position for a while, but they'll get used to it.

I play, my mind drifting off while my body dances with the violin.

When the song ends and I slowly resurface, I don't open my eyes. I want to stay in this space for a while longer. Alistair doesn't say anything. Maybe he knows that any sound would destroy the peace that's been building over the past few minutes.

I've not felt this happy in a long time. It's crazy, I thought playing the violin would make me sad. Instead, I feel bliss, a deep calm that's healing wounds rather than ripping them open.

I stay in this beautiful state of mind for a while longer, then I open my eyes. Alistair is looking at me, in exactly the same position as when I started playing.

"Thank you," he whispers.

I smile. "Thank you."

I hand him the violin and he carefully lays it back onto its old place on the piano.

"You're welcome to come here and play whenever you want," he says softly. He's close suddenly, his breath tickling my cheek. We've not been this close to each other before. He's always kept his distance, and so have I. I don't want to get too attached to these men, but right now, I wish he would close the space between us. His eyes are pools of molten glacier water, cool and strong. I could drown in them and would still be happy.

He stays there, so close it would only take a small stumble to fall against him. Into his arms. Would he hold me like he did the violin, or would he push me away?

I don't want to find out. Neither possibility would be good for my broken little heart.

He seems to come to the same conclusion and steps back, averting his eyes.

"I need to work," he says, his voice a little husky. "See you later."

He almost runs from the room and I'm left feeling strangely empty and relieved at the same time. I look at the violin and smile. I think I've made a new friend.

♥

I've slept in. How the hell did that happen? For weeks, my sleep has been restless, if I got any at all. Sleeping outside is dangerous, and whenever someone walked past, I'd wake up, ready to run. In hospital, I only slept because of the drugs they gave me, and that sleep wasn't as restful as normal sleep.

Now though, I'm wide awake, not tired at all, and without the lingering taste of bad dreams in my mouth. I have a feeling that this day is going to be good.

I take the phone from my nightstand to check the time. 9:21. I've really slept quite a long time, almost twelve hours.

There are two unread messages.

Gladiator: *A nurse will come at 10 am to help you shower and to check on you.*

I smile. As much as I don't like being reliant on someone to wash me, it's a lot better to have a nurse do it than the three men.

The second message is from Alistair.

Genius: *We were called to work early, there's breakfast in the fridge, help yourself. Should be back by lunch time. Music room is all yours.*

My smile widens at the last sentence. Yes, I think I might take him up on that.

I limp to the wardrobe and put on a warm dressing gown, before taking my crutches and heading towards the kitchen. There's no use in putting on proper clothes if I'm going to have a shower in half an hour anyway.

In the fridge, a bowl of fruit salad is waiting for me. Someone must have been up early to prepare it, or maybe late last night after I'd gone to bed? My bet is on Luther. He's the one making sure everything in this house is as homely and welcoming as possible. He'll make a great husband one day. Now, if he also likes to clean... perfect. She'll be one lucky lady.

I take the bowl and sit on one of the tall chairs at the breakfast bar, crutches by my side. The fruit is delicious, just the right balance between crunchy and juicy. There's some cinnamon in it too, I believe. Right at this moment, following Ben's invitation seems like a good decision. I have a roof over my head, as much food as I want, some friendly company and even new clothes. And a phone.

I send a quick message to all three of them.

Em: *Thanks for breakfast. Hope work isn't too stressful.*

Mere seconds later, I get a reply.

Superman: *Not stressful, just boring. Been in meetings since 7 am.*

Genius: *You shouldn't be texting while in a meeting.*

Superman: *Right back at yourself.*

Gladiator: *I'm bored.*

I chuckle.

Em: *Are you all in the same meeting?*

Genius: *Yes. I think even our boss is bored.*

Gladiator: *At least she brought brownies. I'll try and save you some, Em.*

I smile. He's so cute. Jess would have never done anything like that. No, I shouldn't compare him to Jess, not any of them. They're not my boyfriends. They're something very different. I think we're at the stage between acquaintances and friends, except that wouldn't usually include living together. It's such a strange situation. Not one I'd ever thought to find myself being in. But now that I am, I think I'm quite enjoying it. Definitely better than living out on the streets, and miles better than living with that bitch of an ex. I have no idea what she's doing, and I don't want to know.

Genius: *There's a laptop inside the living room table, if you want some entertainment.*

I'm not sure what to do with that information. I've mainly used my old laptop for work, for finding contracts and translating whatever my clients gave me. I'm not a gamer and I'm not on any social networks. I guess I could look at the news or something like that. Maybe watch a film. But I might just play the violin, and then snuggle up with a book. It's weird not having anything to do. No need to find food and shelter, no need to work.

I look at the bathrobe I'm wearing. It's an expensive one, I recognised the label. Okay, I really should work. I need to pay off my debts. I don't want to be indebted to these guys. Keeping my independence is my main goal just now, and even though my broken leg isn't allowing me much of that, I still want to work towards it. Yes, I'm going to see if I can do some translating.

The doorbell makes me jump. It's a loud, ear-shattering ring that reverberates through the entire house. Even the dead would wake from this sound. I rub my ears and limp towards the door, just down the corridor from the kitchen. There's a peephole and I take a quick look at whoever is waiting outside. It's a woman, quite old, maybe in her late fifties, wearing a thick black coat and a large bag swung over her shoulder. Her hair is almost entirely grey but there are two bright purple highlights towards the front.

I open the door and smile at her, but she doesn't smile back.

"Emily Malone?" she asks, her voice bored. Seems she doesn't really want to be here. Great. An unwilling nurse who's going to have to help me shower. I think neither of us is going to enjoy this, but after smelling my armpits this morning, I know it's necessary.

"Yes, come in," I croak, my voice barely cooperating.

She follows me inside, seeming impatient with how slow I am. Well, excuse me, I have a broken foot and am moving on crutches. She's a nurse, she should be understanding. Maybe she's having a bad day.

"Let's go straight to the bathroom," she says, no, she demands. I nod and lead her towards my little studio. The bathroom there isn't very big, but the other ones are on the first floor, and I really don't feel like hopping up the stairs.

Once we've reached the door to the bathroom, she puts her bag on the floor and looks at me, frowning.

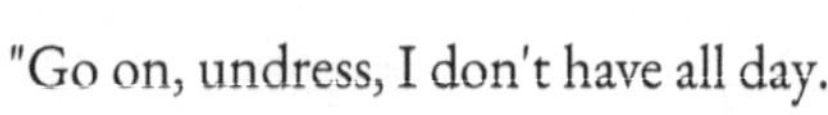

"Go on, undress, I don't have all day."

She rummages in her bag and pulls out a foldable plastic stool, a bottle that could either be shower gel or shampoo, and a pair of gloves. This is going to be torture.

Twenty minutes later, she's gone and I'm feeling humiliated. She didn't just hold the shower sprinkler over me, she also took a washcloth and rubbed it between my legs, under my arms and all over my body, as if I was an invalid and couldn't do it myself. My cheeks are still burning with embarrassment. How dare she! I wish I'd stood up to her while she was there, but no, I was too shy. Fucking shy. I need to be stronger. I need to remember that I survived weeks on the streets. I can't go back to being the old, weak me. I'm no longer nice, sweet Emily. I'm Em now, strong, confident Em.

I run my hands through my wet hair. She had a hairdryer in her bag, but didn't bother offering it to me. I've searched the drawers in the studio, but haven't found one, so I'm going to have to let it air dry. I shrug and twist it in a knot so it doesn't stick to my neck.

I could do with a hot chocolate. Comfort food.

I check my phone in the hope of the guys saying that they'll be back soon, but there are no new messages.

I huff. Already I'm becoming reliant on them. I'm old enough to make myself a hot chocolate. Hell, I've run a household for years. It's just... I hate rummaging around someone else's kitchen. Luther probably has a set order for where everything is, and I don't want to interfere with that.

So instead of getting a drink, I head to the living room and pull a random book from the shelf. It's a thriller, something about mutilated bodies being found in the Siberian tundra. Not my usual cup of tea, but why not? I cuddle up on the sofa, making sure my leg is elevated, and cover myself in a fluffy red blanket I found draped over the armchair. I've got my phone next to me, just in case one of the guys messages. I'm tempted to send them a quick text myself, but what am I supposed to say? That I miss them? That I'm bored? That I feel lonely?

No, I'm going to behave like a grown up. Like an independent woman who isn't craving someone to be here and hold her.

# Eleven

"Let her sleep."

"But I made lunch."

"You can reheat it."

I smile and open my eyes. "I'm awake." My voice almost fails but I think the message got through.

I'm curled up on the sofa, warm and cosy beneath my blanket. How did I manage to fall asleep again after sleeping in this morning? I've always been an early riser, rarely waking up after eight. And here I am taking a nap. That's so not me.

"Are you feeling alright?" Luther looks down at me, frowning. "Are you ill?"

I shake my head and immediately regret it. My neck hurts. I need to remember to communicate with hand signals. Yuck.

"Did the nurse come?" Ben walks over and goes on his knees in front of the sofa so that his head is on my level.

I suppress a shudder and hold up a hand.

Ben smiles. "Good. Are you hungry?"

"Beef stew," Luther whispers from above. "And chocolate pudding for dessert. A little bird has told me that you're a bit of a chocolate addict."

I lift my hand higher in confirmation, but it's actually quite a lot of effort. I'm tired, *really* tired. I could do with another nap. Food doesn't sound as appealing as sleeping, even if there's chocolate pudding.

I close my eyes and wrap my blanket a little closer, ready to go back into the comforting embrace of sleep.

"Em?" Ben asks softly. "Are you not feeling well?"

I'm too tired to even respond. Someone is touching my forehead, but I'm already drifting off, dreaming of chocolate pudding.

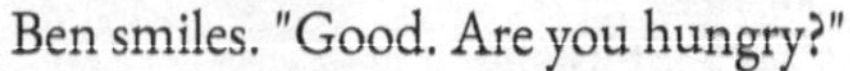

Hands on my shoulders. Grabbing me. Shaking me. No, not again. I can't let him get close. He's going to kill me, he said so. I need to get him off me. I struggle against his grip, but there's something around me that prevents me from moving. Has he bound me?

"Em, calm down, it's just me."

I hear him and yet I don't. It takes a long time for his words to make sense, and by then, my fingernails have finally found somewhere to bite into. He groans in shock and the grip on me lessens.

I open my eyes.

Fuck.

Alistair is standing bent over me, a bloody streak

running down his right arm. His eyes are fixed on me, but he's not looking angry. Is that concern? Surprise? Why does this man have such a poker face? It's not fair.

"Let me see."

A female voice, behind Alistair. I lift my head from the pillow - wait, I'm no longer on the sofa. I'm in bed, my bed in the studio. The lights in the room are on, the chandelier on the ceiling swaying gently in a draught caused by the open door. The curtains are drawn. It must be night. Did I sleep all day?

"You'll be fine, you've had worse," the woman says, her voice melodious with a hint of humour.

Alistair moves a little and reveals the woman behind him. She's stunning, even though she's totally not my type. Pale blond hair falls down her shoulders, so straight that it must have taken her forever to get it that way. She's wearing a little too much makeup for my taste, and it almost overshadows her natural beauty. High cheekbones, long lashes, a voluptuous mouth. She's probably in her forties, but her body is lean and fit.

She pushes Alistair out of the way, grinning. "Next time, I suggest a different way to wake her."

Then she turns to me, smiling. "I'm Charlie. The boys were a wee bit worried about you, so they called me to give you a quick check up. Is that okay with you?"

I must have looked at her a bit confused, because she laughs and points at a name badge pinned to her purple blouse.

"I'm a doctor, sweetie. I don't deal with living people a lot, but I do make exceptions for friends." She lifts my wrists with one hand and takes my pulse. "Any pain?"

I shake my head, then grunt as pain shoots through my neck. Okay, I really need to remember that shaking my head is out of bounds for now.

"No," I wince and she raises a manicured eyebrow.

"She's not supposed to talk," Alistair interrupts. "We've been using hand signals and text messages."

Charlie grins. "You're very cute, you know that, right?"

Somehow, I don't like her calling Alistair cute. It makes me want to push her away from him and the others. Is that me being... possessive? Jealous, even? No, that can't be.

"She's allowed to talk in moderation," she says with a sigh, directed at Alistair. "Just don't shout, sing, that kind of stuff. Now, let me take your blood pressure."

She slides a cuff up my arm and begins to inflate it. When it gets too tight, I suck in a sharp breath, not wanting to complain.

"Too tight?" she asks, frowning. "Sorry, I'm not used to my patients complaining."

Alistair huffs. "That's because they're dead."

Charlie gives me a wink. "That doesn't mean they're not my patients."

"Pathologist?" I ask, my voice no more than a rough whisper.

"I prefer Doctor of the Dead," Charlie says cheerily. "I trained as a doctor, but then noticed it's much more fun if your patients can't talk back at you."

"That's because you're antisocial," Alistair observes.

Charlie turns and gives him the finger. "I'm very social. I talk to my patients every day. It's not my fault that the conversation is rather one sided."

I laugh and they both turn to me.

I'm not quite sure what to say now. Charlie, I think you're a funny person and maybe I'd even like to be your friend, as long as you don't get too close to the men I'm living with? Nah, I don't think that would work. Instead, I look down at the blood pressure cuff which is still a little too tight.

"Am I healthy?" I ask and Charlie nods.

"You're still healing. Your body is busy knitting your bones back together, so you can't expect to be as strong and energetic as you might usually be. Take it easy, sleep as much as you want, take painkillers when you need them. Basically, behave like this is a holiday."

Alistair chuckles. "Do you always take pills while on holiday?"

Charlie shrugs, but doesn't answer his question. Instead, she slips the blood pressure cuff off my arm and packs it into her black backpack.

"Now, I was promised some chocolate pudding as payment?" She grins and leaves the room, probably heading towards the kitchen.

Alistair stays, his hands in the pockets of his dark, perfectly ironed trousers, looking a little unsure of what to do next.

"Sorry we called her," he finally says. "You were sleeping really deeply and wouldn't wake up. Ben thought you had a bit of a temperature, but it was probably just

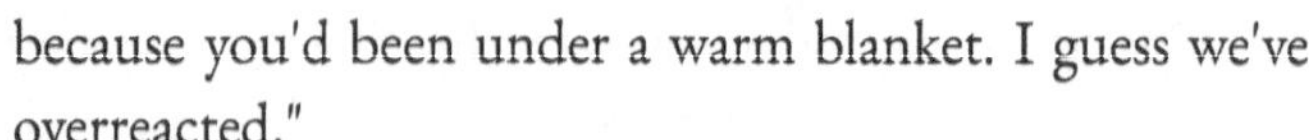

because you'd been under a warm blanket. I guess we've overreacted."

"It's okay." I give him a smile. "But why did you call her and not a normal doctor?"

My voice is hoarse and rough around the edges, but it's good to be able to talk. I hope they're not going to insist on hand signals again anytime soon.

Alistair laughs. "She's someone who doesn't have a social life. When she's not working, she's at home, spending time with her cats. If you need a doctor to come over after hours, she's the person to call. She's a genius, really. Aced all her exams. She could have worked at any hospital she would have liked, but she decided to retrain as a pathologist. I think it suits her, but there were a lot of people who didn't support her decision."

I push back my blanket and sit up. My head is spinning a little, probably because I've been sleeping too long. My limbs feel heavy, but I know I need to move. I can't lay here any longer. And no, it's not because of the chocolate pudding that might be disappearing into Charlie's stomach just now. No, not at all.

"Is there still pudding left?" I ask and Alistair chuckles.

"We saved you some, don't worry. I'm sure Luther is going to make you some hot chocolate as well. But now stop talking. You sound like your voice is about to die a painful death."

I grimace but he's right. Talking hurts. I shouldn't overdo it.

He hands me my crutches and together, we head to

the kitchen. Charlie is sitting there, an empty bowl in front of her.

"Em! How are you feeling?" Ben is by my side as soon as we enter the room. His hair is all over the place, as if he's been running his hands through it a little too often.

"I'm okay," I whisper and he frowns at me.

"No talking."

I sigh and let Alistair explain that the rules have been changed a little. I'm rather grateful to Charlie for that.

I sit next to Charlie and Luther puts a giant bowl of chocolate pudding in front of me. In other households, this would be enough to feed a family, but I don't care. I'm hungry and this is chocolate. No other arguments needed.

I start eating, the velvety texture of the chocolate mousse coating my tongue. I don't look up, completely focused on my food. This is what heaven must feel like.

"She's cute," Charlie mutters as if I wasn't in the room. "Are you going to keep her?"

"Charlie!" Ben growls. "Don't talk about our guest that way."

She doesn't seem to care that she's making him angry. "You need a woman in this household, I've been telling you for years. And she seems to be a perfect match for you."

"I'm right here," I mutter between two spoonfuls of pudding. "And I'm just here until I can get back on my feet."

Silence greets my words.

Then Charlie begins to laugh. "I hope I don't have to start treating you for a severe case of self-delusion. Have you seen how these buffoons look at you? They were so worried that they threatened me until I promised to come and check on you. You won't get rid of them easily, sweetie, no chance."

I let my spoon drop back into my bowl, taken aback.

"That's enough," Alistair says, his voice strangely passive. "I think you should get back to your cats now."

Charlie snickers. "Mark my words, boys. It's obvious that you're into her, so don't waste this chance." She winks at me. "By the way, choosing one of them would be so boring. I say take them all."

This woman is crazy. She gets up and leaves, but not before giving me another wink. I'm left with three speechless men, and I myself don't know what to say either. Such a weird situation. There should be a guidebook for this. How to live with three strangers who've picked you up from the streets. How to not get attached with three kind men who're looking after you in a way that nobody has ever cared for you before.

I sigh and eat the last of my chocolate pudding. I'm so full, but I can't leave any leftovers. That would be a sin against the mighty chocolate gods.

"Good?" Luther asks when I push back the bowl and lean back.

"Very. Thanks."

He takes the bowl and puts it in the dishwasher behind him. Ben and Alistair are standing behind me, not saying anything. I turn around.

"What shall we do now?"

Ben sighs. "I think I could do with a drink. And no, I

don't mean hot chocolate. Something stronger, a lot stronger."

"And me," Alistair agrees and walks to a cabinet in the corner. It turns out to be full of bottles of all shapes and sizes.

"Brandy?" he asks but Ben shakes his head.

"Whisky. The good stuff. Em, want one too?"

I grin. "Whisky? Always."

# Twelve

For the past two days, the guys have been forcing me to sit on the sofa with my leg up, doing nothing but reading, watching tv and listening to music. Alistair showed me some of his favourite video games too, but quickly got frustrated at being beaten by me.

Alistair loves computers. He's got several and, according to Luther, they all have names. As a child, Al's skin was even more sensitive than it is now, so playing in the sunlight resulted in painful rashes. Even now, he spends most of the day inside while the other two do the field work.

"I'm too memorable," he said when I asked why. "Ben blends in everywhere, and Luther in some circles, but with my looks, people keep remembering me when they shouldn't. I can't go around asking questions without being noticed. So instead, I do the coordination from here and let them do all the walking."

So while the other two have been out, Alistair has

been spending time with me. I still don't understand him. He's not been as cold again as he was when I first arrived, but he's got moments when he's curt and distant. After being around him for almost two full days, you'd think that I'd know him better. But no, he's still an enigma. A rather attractive one, I have to admit. We've not been in the music room again together. I've played the violin twice, but he never joined me.

Now though, it finally seems that things are going to change. The guys have called a meeting and I think this is the moment they tell me what work I'm actually going to do for them.

Luther and Ben have cleared the kitchen table. All that remains is a simple manila folder.

"We got your contract approved," Ben says cheerily as he pulls back a chair for me. Seriously, do they teach them at spy school to be such gentlemen?

"Our superiors are happy with our choice in you, so now all you need is to sign."

I take out the contract from the folder. It's at least fifty pages long. Seriously? I'll need all morning to go through that.

"Ben, want to give me a summary again?"

Alistair frowns disapprovingly but Ben grins. "The initial contract is for six months, to be extended at our discretion. Your annual leave allowance and salary can be found on the final page. And yes, we tried to get it as high as possible."

I open the last page and my eyes widen. Hell, I've never been anywhere near that salary before.

"There's a bonus for nights and weekends too."

I look at them. "Seriously? How is this financed? I thought the government has no money?"

Luther chuckles. "We're on the front line of fighting crime. There's money for that."

"Aren't the police the front line?"

"Okay, we're the front-line intelligence. Better?"

I smile innocently. "Front line spies?"

Alistair growls. "Don't use that word in my house." He turns to the other two and shrugs. "I liked her better when she wasn't talking."

I grab the contract and sign at the back. "Too late. Now you're stuck with me."

"And you with us, don't forget that," Ben says with a smile. "And to celebrate our fourth musketeer joining us, I've ordered sushi!"

Luther groans.

"He doesn't like it when we order food," Alistair whispers. "But sushi seems to be the only food he can't cook himself."

"My sushi was excellent," Luther protests.

Ben huffs. "They were too big, too meaty, not sticky enough. They were little abominations rolled in nori."

I watch their bickering with an ache in my chest. They belong together, they're a team. Will I be able to become a part of them? Or will I be the fourth wheel on a three-wheel car?

"We've got your first assignment, Em," Ben announces. He pulls out a slim laptop from below the counter and hands it to me. "We intercepted several letters to one of our Albanian friends." From the way he pronounces 'friends', I'm pretty sure they're quite the opposite. "I need you to translate them; the scans are in the Project Tuna folder."

I snort. "Project Tuna? Seriously?"

"Luther always uses food to name our assignments. Don't remind me of Mission Coronation Chicken."

I laugh as I switch on the laptop. It's sleek, light and looks expensive. Just like the phone they gave me. Damn, these guys have money.

There's only one folder on the desktop and I open it. Ten images of scanned, crumpled letters are waiting for me.

"Why letters? Why don't they write emails?"

"They think they are harder to trace. Which is bullshit," Luther explains. "There's a note at the post office to scan any letters going to this address before passing them on. We've found out quite a few titbits of interesting information through that."

"I'll get on it right away," I announce, glad to finally be able to do something. I don't want to be a scrounger, living on the guys' generosity.

"Thank you," Ben says, looking at his watch. "Lunch should arrive in about two hours. Al, how's Project Broccoli going?"

While they talk about Alistair hacking into someone's bank accounts, I open the first letter. Whoever has written it has terrible handwriting. Deciphering these scrawls will take time, even before I start translating.

I excuse myself, take my crutches and head to the living room to be able to work in quiet. My work as a super spy has begun.

Ben was right, the sushi is excellent. I've not had sushi since... I don't even know. It's been years. I forgot how much I loved that.

For dessert, Ben ordered mochi; sweet, sticky rice cakes. They cling to the top of my mouth in the most delicious way. I love Luther's cooking, but this is just... amazing.

After lunch, we sit together, everyone lost in their own thoughts. I admire how everyone in this household fits together. So far there have been no major arguments. There are a few rules, like everybody cleaning up after themselves, but besides that, the guys seem practiced at living together, better than most couples.

"Do you remember Joanna's reaction to sushi?" Alistair asks suddenly and the other two groan.

"Don't start, we've only just finished eating," Luther complains, making theatrical gagging noises.

"Who's Joanna?" I ask, a tiny voice inside of me begging that it isn't a secret girlfriend. Which makes me question why that would upset me. It was the same with Charlie. I quickly dismiss that thought though. It's that time of the month, of course my hormones are looking for something to latch onto. Like three hot guys sitting around me, for example.

"My ex," Ben sighs.

"No, my ex," Alistair mutters.

"And mine," Luther adds.

"Are you saying that you were all with this one girl? One after the other or... at the same time?"

"Both?" Alistair says, looking at the other two for confirmation. They nod, but stay quiet, while I'm bursting inside with all my curiosity.

"How can that be?" I ask, trying not to sound too eager.

"She was my girlfriend first," Ben explains. "Then she had an affair with Alistair, then Luther. At the same time. Without any of us knowing. When it came to light, she disappeared. We still don't know if she was for real, or someone sent to spy on us. Or even a test from our superiors, but if it was, we definitely failed."

"What a bitch," I curse, surprised by the passion in my voice. I shouldn't be feeling this annoyed at their behalf, surely? And a little disappointed that they didn't share her?

"Yeah, she definitely was that. Ever since, we've been very open about our relationships with each other." Luther sighs. "Not that there's much to talk about at the moment. Three single men, living in a house together like students, with jobs that don't allow them to talk about their work with others. I don't think we're prime relationship material at the moment."

I want to disagree - and again, I can't believe that I almost protested. What the heck is wrong with me? Sure, I've been with guys before, but always just a short fling. I've only been in long-term relationships with girls. Two, to be exact, and both ended badly. So why am I drooling over three men?

"When did Joanna leave?" I ask curiously.

"About ten months ago. This house has been without a female visitor since then. You're the first woman we've had to stay with us in almost a year," Ben says, only to correct himself a second later. "But only to stay platonically, of course, totally platonically. Not like Joanna, not at all."

Luther laughs. "Better stop there, Ben. You don't want to scare our guest."

"I'm not easily scared," I protest.

"No?" Suddenly serious Ben is back, the investigator with the piercing eyes who talked to me in that cafe. The one who thinks he can tell truth from lies.

I grin. "Two truths, one lie. I'm scared of octopi. I'm scared of wedding dresses. I'm scared of fire."

"Can we guess as well?" Alistair pipes up enthusiastically.

"Go ahead. One guess each."

"What does the winner get?" he asks with an innocent smirk.

"What do you want?"

"A hug."

I sigh. Men. "Okay then, tell me your guesses."

Ben has been staring at me while I came up with my three statements. In fact, I don't think he's blinked at all. He's still studying me, but his gaze has turned from curious to something else. Predatory.

"I'll go for octopi as the lie," Luther decides.

"Nah, I think it's wedding dresses," Alistair argues.

Ben still hasn't said anything. I'm starting to squirm under his scrutiny. Finally, he smiles. "Fire."

Wow, three different answers. And it's such a pity that one of them is, therefore, right.

I get up and limp over to Ben, spreading my arms

wide. "Sir, you are the winner," I announce, making him laugh. He pulls me close and gently hugs me, then wraps his arms around my chest until I'm forced to sit on his lap, my legs straddling his waist. His fingers drum on my shoulder blades; it tickles. I lean against his chest and his grip tightens. He starts running his hands over my back, circling slowly. With each circle, they reach a lower point on my spine. The anticipation of him soon touching my bum is making me shiver. I press against him, not wanting this hug to end. And judging from the hard bulge pressing against my stomach, neither does he.

He rests his chin on the top of my head as he slides his hands under my jumper. They're cold and I shiver again, both from the cold and the sensations running through my body. This is turning into more than just a hug. And I know the other two are watching, but right now, I don't care. We could be standing in the middle of a busy road and I wouldn't want him to stop. He's exploring my back with his hands, while rubbing against my front with his chest, making my nipples harden. I know without looking that they're showing through the bra. I ache to be touched. It's been so long.

Should I really be doing this? If we continue, there will be no return. So far, I've been a guest, a platonic one, as they pointed out. If I start something with one of them... what if it ends badly? What if I'll have to leave because of it? Is this worth it?

He lowers his head until his lips are on the nape of my neck, gently hovering above my skin. His breath is hot. Instead of touching me, he gently blows on my skin, starting on my right shoulder and working his way down towards my décolleté. Okay, this is definitely worth it. I don't care about his hands still running over my back, I want to feel his lips on my body, on my mouth, everywhere. A slight moan escapes me and a chuckle rises from his chest. Slowly, very slowly, he opens his mouth and licks over the soft skin above my breasts, where my jumper ends. Now I wish I had put on something more revealing. Something with more... access.

Suddenly, he places both hands on my bum and pulls me even closer against him. I can no longer ignore this erection. He knows I can feel it; he knows how I affect him.

So far, my hands have been hugging him, not moving. I was too busy trying to control myself - ripping off his clothes in front of the other two didn't seem like a good idea. But I no longer care. I claw his back, showing him that I want to play. That I want more. I don't want to be passive. I want all of him.

I move back a tiny bit, just enough to squeeze one hand in between us. He groans when I place it on the bulge between his legs. I want to free him.

I fumble with the button on his jeans. Why can't men just wear jeans with velcro? So much easier to open...

"Let me," he whispers hoarsely and takes his hands off my bum, helping me open his trousers. I slide a hand in, gently embracing his manhood. He's rather large, and rock-hard. I'm not used to anything bigger than my ex's strap-on, so this is going to be interesting... if we do it. Maybe he doesn't want to. Maybe he thinks what the rational part of my mind is screaming just now: we've only just met; we're in the same room as two others; if I sleep with him, does that make me someone giving sex in return for a bed? But then he gently lowers his hand and touches me between my legs, and all those worries disappear.

I gently stroke the silky skin on his cock, revelling in the groans this produces. I'm exploring, experimenting, while he massages my mound through the fabric of my trousers. I can feel myself growing wet. Gripping his hair with one hand, I pull him closer until our lips meet. Finally.

"If you two don't get a room, I'll come and join you," Luther growls from the other end of the kitchen table.

I open my mouth to respond, but Ben takes this as an invitation to press past my lips with his tongue. He enters my mouth, playfully nudging my tongue out of the way. I moan, fire racing through my body. I need more. I wrap my arms around his back, needing more of his touch, his mouth, his hands.

He breaks the kiss, leaving me breathless. "Take off your shirt," he whispers huskily, and I don't even think about it, I just do it. My nipples are pressing hard against the silky fabric of my bra. Alistair bought it for me; black and covered with tiny roses. I wonder if he ever imagined me wearing it in front of him. Right now, I want it off my body.

Someone reads my mind and unclasps it from behind. I turn, only for my mouth to be met by hard, demanding lips. Luther has joined us. I give in to his kiss, opening for him. He isn't as playful as Ben, he's impatient and firm. While he's pushing into my mouth, my bra is slid down my arms until I'm naked from the waist up. Ben sucks in his breath.

I close my eyes, going with the flow. Hands are touching me, my breasts, my nipples, gently squeezing, rubbing, pulling. A mouth on my throat, nibbling on my skin. My trousers are being pulled down and with the guys' help, I slip them over my cast and step out of them, held in strong arms that won't let me fall. A finger slides past the fabric of my panties and enters me from below. I quiver, my legs no longer able to stand. Luther pulls back from the kiss and I breathe, still not opening my eyes.

"Let's go somewhere more comfortable," he whispers, and picks me up as if I weigh nothing. Snuggling against him, he carries me into one of the guys' bedrooms. The others are following us, breathing just as heavily as I am.

# Thirteen

L uther puts me down on the bed and rips off my panties. Without a word, I spread my legs wide. It's like a dream in which I do things I would never do in reality. Inviting three men to touch me. Wanting them to fill me. Craving their touch.

"Are you sure about this?" Ben whispers into my ear, and I know that he refers to the assault. But right now, my memories are silent, all that's alive in my mind is the desire for them.

"Yes," I whisper, opening my eyes to look into his beautiful brown gaze. "I want you."

"We can stop at any time," he promises, but to me, it sounds almost like a threat. I don't want them to stop. They haven't even started.

Ben leans down and kisses me passionately. I close my eyes again, wanting to feel every tiny touch without my vision interfering. Ben's lips on mine are causing sparks to explode in my mind. Our tongues dance in harmony, circling each other, embracing lovingly.

Something wet is at my nipples - no, it's one of the guys taking it into his mouth. He's sucking gently, the puckered skin stretching as my nipple is elongated. His tongue flicks over the top of it and I arch my back, wanting more. Luckily, they get the message. A second later, my other nipple gets the same treatment. All three guys have their mouths on me, sucking on my nipples, kissing me deeply. I moan as I feel a hand slowly parting my folds, rubbing my bud in small circles. I reach out and encourage them to go further. Alistair chuckles as I guide him deeper until his finger slips into me with a satisfying sound. I am so wet; I can feel my wetness running down my arse. I'm aching to feel one of them inside me. Alistair moves his finger in and out, exploring, turning, then adding a second. I stretch, thrusting my hips down to meet him. I want him deeper, but his fingers aren't long enough. I groan in frustration, and Ben nips my lower lip in response. He starts to suckle on it, driving me crazy. They are all making me crazy with their foreplay.

"Please, hurry up," I gasp, making them all laugh.

"I didn't expect her to be so impatient," Luther grins, beginning to massage my bud while Alistair's fingers are still stretching me inside. Goosebumps are forming on my skin, making it even more sensitive.

"Who is going to go first?" Alistair asks, and I know it's a question for both the guys and me. But I don't want to choose. I want them all. Am I greedy? Definitely. Am I crazy for doing this, for wanting them, for not listening to that insistent voice in my head that's telling me to stop? Oh yes.

Ben stops nibbling on my lips and leaves his place by

my side. I can hear him take off his trousers. He's been hard for so long, he must be desperate for release. Remembering how his cock felt in my hand, I open my legs even further, inviting him in. A condom wrapper falls to the floor - I didn't expect anything less from Ben. His tip touches me gently, as if asking for permission, before he pushes in, past the muscles resisting slightly, until he fills me fully. He's big, stretching me until it's almost painful, but in the best possible way.

He begins to move slowly, making me moan in pleasure. Alistair takes Ben's former place and gently kisses my lips, rubbing over mine with his. He's not using his tongue like the others; instead, he pulls back and then presses hard against my mouth again and again, teasing me, not letting me feel him properly. It's frustrating and incredibly hot at the same time.

Luther cups my breasts in his large hands, beginning to massage them with a tight grip. He's not one to be gentle, and I like that about him. He's uncompromising, steadfast, strong. Right now, I could kiss him for what he does to my nipples - but my mouth is already being occupied by Alistair.

I hear a zipper open and almost simultaneously, a second one. Luther's hands disappear from my breasts and I groan in disappointment.

He chuckles. "Stretch out your arms, beautiful."

I do as he says, spreading my arms until my wrists are at the edges of the mattress.

"Good girl." I can hear the smile in his voice.

He guides my right hand until I can feel his cock, thick-veined and hard. I grip it and have trouble fitting my hand around him. He is going to hurt. And feel so good.

I begin to rub his cock up and down, rotating my thumb on his tip, spreading the drop of pre-cum that's warm and sticky against my skin.

While Ben's rhythm is getting faster, grinding my arse against the satin sheet, Alistair stops his kiss only to lick my fingers a moment later, taking them into his mouth one by one. I didn't think it could feel this good. His mouth is like a warm cave I could curl up in - then his cock is in my wet hand and I know why he did it. I start pumping him, my hand slick from his kisses. He is not as thick as Luther or Ben, but longer.

Ben is pounding into me, and with every thrust, I squeeze the other two cocks in my hands until we all groan in unison. Alistair bends forward, taking one of my nipples into his mouth again. I arch my back, making it easier for him to gently take it between his teeth and pull. A beautiful pain runs through me and collides with the pleasure in my core. I am close to coming. White lights are exploding in front of my closed eyelids. Every nerve is firing, and I don't think I've ever felt this *much* before. Luther runs his hands over my body until one of them reaches between my legs. He spreads my folds and puts a finger on my clit, rubbing as Ben thrusts in and out of me.

I can't take it any longer. With a scream of bliss, I explode, my muscles wrapping tight around Ben, milking him as he comes in me. I hold onto their cocks for dear life, riding wave after wave of shivering pleasure. Ben pushes deep into me, remaining there, not leaving me as the orgasm continues to shake my body.

When my breath finally slows down a little, Ben moves back, sliding out of me. I open my eyes and am rewarded with his proud smile.

"Still ready for more?" Luther whispers hoarsely, and I nod, unable to speak. The intensity of this is freezing my brain, not letting my thoughts be occupied by anything but euphoria.

He takes Ben's place, hurriedly puts on a condom and pushes into me without warning, claiming his stake on me. He's not gentle, but I don't expect him to be. His groans are becoming primal as his hard cock opens me again and again. Ben covers my mouth with his lips, letting me taste him while Luther rams into me. My grip on Alistair's cock is getting weaker, but it will be his turn soon. I want them all.

Ben grasps my shoulders, pushing me against Luther, making him enter me deeper than I thought possible. With a cry and one final strong thrust, Luther comes, gripping my thighs tightly, holding me in place while his cock twitches in me. Alistair has started drawing wet lines on my belly with his tongue, working his way downwards. Luther pulls out, and Alistair's tongue takes his place, lapping up my juices that are by now spread all over. He tickles my entrance before sucking on my nub, almost bringing me to another climax.

"Fuck me," I gasp. I want to come when he's in me. He needs to complete the circle.

He licks me once more and I want to complain again,

but then he promises, "Next time," in a tone that makes me shiver in anticipation. I hear him put on a condom, then he enters me and all I can see are stars. He takes my hands and pulls me up until I'm half sitting on the edge of the bed, him buried within me. He takes me into his arms, hugging me against his chest. I wrap my legs around him, driving his cock deeper into me as he begins to move. This is a more intimate fuck; he's taking it slower than the other two, but it's no less intense. I grind my hips against him, relishing in the knowledge that the other two are watching us. I don't recognise this new exhibitionist me, but she's taken root inside and is not going to leave anytime soon.

My nipples are rubbing against the coarse fabric of his shirt while my bum lifts off the bed with every thrust. I'm close, so close. Hanging onto him in desperate ecstasy, I come, the orgasm rippling through my body. Alistair continues to fuck me, harder and harder, and he drives my climax even higher. My breathing is heavy and strands of hair stick to my forehead, but it doesn't end, he rams into me again, and again, one final time, then he comes, shaking as his cock twitches in me.

Spent, I sink back, his arms gently guiding me down onto the mattress.

I open my eyes and return the smiles of my three men.

# Fourteen

A kiss on my forehead wakes me from a deep slumber. I stretch my arms - and am wide awake when my hand hits something and it shouts "ouch!".

Alistair is rubbing his cheek which I apparently hit. He's grinning though, which makes me feel less bad about it.

"Sorry," I mumble, still working on my brain-mouth coordination.

"From now on I'll wear protective armour when I come to wake you," he announces. I smile, not so much about his bad joke, but rather about the fact that he made it sound like he's going to wake me up again in the future. Often. Which means I'm going to be with him and the others for a while. Something warm and fluffy expands inside me at that thought. Could this become my home?

"I just wanted to tell you that I need to leave. We got a lead and the other two have already gone to check it out. This could be a breakthrough, so we need all hands on deck. I sent you some audio files to translate, they should be on your desktop. Could you look at them while we're gone, and text me a summary of what they say?"

Now fully alert, I sit up, the duvet sliding down - and I notice that I'm still naked. Alistair laughs and leans forward, taking one nipple into his mouth and gives it a gentle suck.

"Maybe we can play later?" he asks as he pulls back with a look of regret.

I shiver in anticipation, and the regret in his eyes turns into desire.

"Yes, and you can fulfil your promise," I respond, my nipples hardening at the thought of having him between my legs again.

"You will see, I always keep my promises."

With a quick kiss on my lips, he leaves, and a moment later, I can hear the main door fall shut. I'm alone. Which, with all the naughty thoughts running through my mind, is a pity.

Quickly pulling on some clothes, I go in search of my laptop, and find it on the kitchen table, next to a glass of orange juice, a stack of pancakes and a massive bottle of maple syrup that has become my best friend in the past few days. I've probably used up half of it by myself. Maple syrup is second only to hot chocolate.

There are five files waiting for me. Not wanting to waste any time, I start listening to the first while having my breakfast. It's a conversation in Albanian, and the audio quality is pretty bad. I'm going to have to listen to this more than once to write a proper transcript. I sigh and get to work.

*A: "How many?"*

*B: "Twelve. One was lost on route. Two are not in the best condition."*

*A: "I want to see them before I pay."*

*B: "I'll have them brought to you tonight. One says she is untouched."*

*A: "Bring her to me also. I've got a buyer interested in that."*

*B: [laughs] "Who isn't interested in those? If I could afford it, I'd take her myself. Do you want them brought here?"*

*A: "Don't be stupid. Too public. I'll be at the warehouse all night. Take them there. And tell one of your girls to get them ready for inspection."*

The recording ends in crackles. Their voices make me shudder. So cold, so... detached. No emotion at all. But that must be a requirement to work in human trafficking.

Alistair hasn't given me a date for when this was recorded. I hope it was earlier today. I hope those girls haven't been sold yet.

I send the transcript to the guys, hoping that it contains useful information.

I make myself a cup of tea and start with the next. It's in Russian this time, and I only understand a few words. It must have been recorded at a party or in a club; there's loud music in the background and too many voices to filter out. I play with the audio settings, trying to reduce the noise. Even so, I only get that they're talking about whisky and what distilleries to visit on a trip up to the north of Scotland.

I dutifully make a note of what I've heard, but unless

they're using code words, I don't think this conversation will be of much use.

The third is Russian again, a couple having an argument about him sleeping with someone else. It's quite entertaining to listen to, but again, not very useful. I make an inner note to ask the guys where they get these recordings from.

Two more to go. It's time for a hot chocolate. Alistair's super-shiny coffee machine has a function for that. It's not as good as when Luther makes one from scratch, but it will do to get me through the rest of the task. Other people need caffeine, I need chocolate.

The fourth recording makes me shudder. It's the sound of women whispering frantically in a language I can't identify. It could be something Asian, but it's definitely not one I can translate. But I don't need to understand them to hear the panic in their voice. I wonder if these are the women the Albanians talked about. But why would the guys have a recording of them? How would they get it? Did they find the women already? Maybe this is for an old mission... but Alistair said it was important to get it done immediately. I send a quick text to him; maybe he knows other interpreters who can help.

The fifth sound file is man A again, but he's talking to someone new with a strong accent, not a native Albanian speaker. There are others in the background, but they're too quiet to understand.

*C: I'm running out of Q. [I've checked it several times, but I believe he means the letter Q]*

*A: Not my problem.*

*C: Oh, but it is. You get them hooked on it, it's your problem. When will you have more?*

*A: I told you, it's not my problem. Find your own supplier.*

*[sound of a scuffle]*

*C: Give me a name and I'll leave. Trust me, you don't want to make me angry.*

*A: Fuck you. I've got stuff on you that would destroy you. Don't threaten me. May the magpie drink from your brains [Albanian expression = threat]*

*C: Looks like we're at a standoff.*

*[a clicking sound]*

*C: I'll take the dark one for insurance. I want two kilos of Q at my doorstep tonight.*

I send the transcript to the guys (my colleagues, I repeat in my head). A second later, my phone rings. It's Ben.

"Good work," he says without a greeting. "I liked the magpie thing."

"Albanians have some very colourful curses," I explain.

"You can tell me some tonight, I might need them in the future. Alistair has managed to hack into one of their laptops and is recording something for you now. You'll have it in your emails in a few minutes. I need you to tell me immediately what it says. We don't need a transcript, just a quick translation so we know whether to call in the cavalry."

Wow, that sounds serious. "No problem. I'll get it to you as soon as."

He hangs up and I bite my lip while waiting for the email to arrive. This is exciting, in a significant kind of way. I might be helping to save lives. This is so much better than translating birth certificates and love letters.

With a bing, the email arrives and I open the attached file. It's only a minute in length, so this won't take long.

I listen to it, and with every second, panic spreads through my body. I grab the phone and dial Ben's number, willing him to answer, but it rings out. Same with the others' phones.

"Fuck," I curse, and send them a text instead, hoping that they'll see it.

Em: *It's a trap. Get out of there!*

I limp back and forth through the kitchen, trying to calm myself, clutching my phone in case one of them calls. This can't be happening. What if they caught them? What would they do to my guys?

I'm thinking of calling the police, but what would I tell them? I don't know who exactly they work for, where they are, if what they're doing is sanctioned. I run my hands through my tangled hair, desperately hoping that none of the possible scenes running through my head will come true. I need them. And I care for them. A lot.

I feel like punching a wall, or someone, preferably one of those bastards that I heard on the recording. They were laughing about the 'three idiots sneaking around the building' and how they would walk into their trap as planned. I still can't get my head around it. My guys are clever. They would spot a trap, right? They wouldn't walk blindly into a house without taking precautions?

"Fuck!" I shout again, grab the empty mug next to my

computer and throw it against the wall. It breaks with a satisfying crunch. Shards fly to the ground, but I don't care.

That's when someone turns the key in the front door. They are back! I take my crutches and the phone - and a text arrives.

Genius: *We've noticed. They know where we live. Don't open the door. Hide.*

I look around the room, wide-eyed, trying to find somewhere to hide. Whatever they are doing here, they won't be interested in the kitchen, right? But all the cabinets are too small for me. Behind the curtains... No, they'd see me. Panicked, I limp out of the kitchen into the hallway, hoping that they don't have a key and need a moment to break into the house. There's a storage closet at the end of the hall where they keep their cleaning stuff. It might be too obvious, but I've got no choice. There's no time to look for a better hiding place.

The closet is small, but there's a flimsy curtain inside, separating a row of shelves from the rest of it. No idea who came up with the idea of putting a curtain into a tiny room that is only used for storage, but right now, I'm incredibly thankful to whoever it was.

I hide my crutches behind the hoover and crawl into the space below the bottom shelf. It's a tight squeeze, but I'm small. I curse the cast that prevents me from taking a more comfortable position. Instead I'm half-crouching, half-lying, hoping that the darkness and curtain will conceal me.

I stop breathing as heavy footsteps echo through the corridor. There must be at least five or six of them. I can hear doors open all around me; they've split up and are searching the house. For what? Documents perhaps? Evidence the guys have collected?

Nobody knows I'm living here with them at the moment, so it can't be me. I'm safe, as long as they don't find me.

My phone display lights up.

Gladiator: *I'm coming.*

Em: *What about the others?*

No reply.

Now I'm really bloody scared.

Footsteps are coming closer. The closet is at the end of the corridor, but the hallway continues to the left, leading to my little studio flat. Fuck. When they see my clothes, they'll know that the guys don't live alone. Maybe it won't interest them, but maybe they'll think it'll give them leverage.

I don't dare to breathe as someone stops in front of the closet door.

"Aleks, we found it!" a man shouts from afar in heavily accented English. Please Aleks, go back, go to your friends and then piss off.

"Just a minute, there's more this way," Aleks yells back in Albanian. Only a flimsy wooden door keeps us apart. Please don't open it. Don't look. You're not interested in this closet. Right now, magic would come in handy.

Finally, he walks away, but not back towards the guy's living quarters, but into the other part of the house. He'll be in my flat any moment.

And true, a moment later he's back in front of my

closet, shouting. "There's a chick living with them. She's got a wheelchair in her room, so maybe she's here somewhere. Search the place!"

Damn, the wheelchair. I've not used it since Ben brought me home from the hospital as I've not left the house. We should have taken it back to the hospital; I'm strong enough to walk on crutches now.

"Out you come, little mouse," Aleks taunts loudly in perfect English. "Don't make the cat come and get you!"

I'm trying to persuade myself that he doesn't actually know that I'm still in here.

"There's a laptop in the kitchen which is still on," a third guy shouts and comes closer. Now there are two men standing in front of my little hiding place. And how could I be so stupid as to leave the laptop on? Granted, I had to get out of there really quickly, but still, what a fucking dumb mistake.

The door to the closet opens, letting light into the dim room. Two pairs of combat boots peek out from under the curtain. I am so screwed.

The curtain is pulled aside – they've found me.

"Hello little mouse." Aleks grins down at me. He's a large man wearing thick rimmed glasses that make his cruel eyes even more intense. His shaved head is covered in a thin sheen of sweat. Behind him, a lanky guy is leering happily as if he's just made the catch of the month. I cower against the wall, but there's no way to escape now. I'm well and truly trapped.

I just hope Luther will be here soon.

# Fifteen

I have to give it to them, these bastards are experts in ropework. My arms and legs are tied to a chair in the centre of the living room. They didn't abduct me... yet. That gives me a tiny bit of hope. Luther said he was on the way, and hopefully the others are with him.

They've removed the scarf I've been wearing around my neck, exposing the bruises that tell the story of the attack that had me end up living with the guys. Aleks gave them an appreciative look, as if he was inspecting a fellow artist's work. My leg is throbbing painfully; I think they squashed part of the cast when they pulled me out of the closet. I struggled like a good little hostage, but it was futile from the very beginning. I can't even stand properly without my crutches, let alone defend myself or run.

"What are you?" Aleks muses, scrutinising me curiously. "Their colleague? Assistant? Whore?"

I spit in his face. Granted, not the smartest move, but nobody calls me a whore without repercussions.

My head is thrown to one side as he backhands me. Wiping the spit off his cheek, he grins dangerously.

"You've just lost any restraint I might have shown. Now, I asked you a question."

I look at him, trying to put as much defiance into my stare as I can. I won't tell him anything. Not that I know much, but I don't give in to bullies. I've done that in the past, I've learned my lesson.

"How did they find us?"

His question is followed by another slap. I can feel the iron taste of blood in my mouth.

I don't reply. He won't get the satisfaction.

"How much do they know?"

Another slap.

"What are you to them?" Slap.

"How many of them are there?" Slap.

"Are you their whore?"

Slap.

Anger is burning in me, mixing with the pain of my hurting cheeks. Don't say anything. They won't stop, even if you do tell them.

"Who are they working for? The government? The mafia?"

Slap.

I'm relieved to find out that they don't actually know as much as I thought they did.

"Are there more than those three idiots?"

Slap.

My neck hurts from my head being thrown to the side and my cheeks are burning. There is more blood in my mouth now, and I feel a trickle of it running down my left cheek where his ring cut my skin.

"Maybe we should start making this a little more fun." He leers at me, and the other men around him step forward, clearly looking forward to this.

"How about we cut off a few of those clothes? We'd quite like to see more of their little slut."

I shiver, memories flooding me. The room is becoming a distant place, the people in it like shadows. The homeless guy is suddenly standing in front of me, putting his hands around my throat once more. His hands are everywhere, he's got many, I don't see them, but they're touching me; my breasts, between my legs, burying his fingernails in my sensitive flesh. Tears are running down my face and I try to get away, but I'm tied to a chair, helpless, exposed. The man - one of them, one of the many - is smiling at the sight of my tears, and wipes them away with a fat finger. It's not a gentle gesture; it's the promise of more pain and humiliation.

Someone grips my chin and pulls me towards them, forcing his stinking lips against mine. I fight, pressing my lips together tightly, not letting him enter, but he bites and slaps me and someone else punches me in the stomach. I gasp and my mouth opens, and then his tongue is in there and I bite, he shouts, more slaps, more punches, footsteps, doors slamming, shouts, shots.

*Shots.*

My bonds are loosened, my body falls forwards, into waiting arms.

I'm on the ground, being gently rocked, my hair being stroked.

"I'm so sorry," someone whispers, "we should never have left you alone."

I'm floating, the thought of being safe slowly permeating my scattered mind. Safe. I thought I was safe before. Then I suddenly wasn't. I'll never be safe. There will always be people who want to hurt me.

"Get an ambulance!" the man holding me shouts, and I cuddle against him, wanting him to protect me from all the sound and chaos.

I'm shivering, remembering that my clothes are lying in a destroyed heap on the floor.

Someone else comes, wraps me in a soft blanket, then I'm returned to the warm arms that rock me gently, making me feel at peace.

"Talk to me, sweetheart," he says, but it's too much effort. My mouth is bleeding and my cheeks have started to throb painfully. Everything is blurry, the world is foggy and unclear, but as long as those arms are around me, it's fine.

"What did they do?" A third voice, familiar. Ben. I weakly stretch out an arm, wanting him here, holding me. He is safe. I trust him.

He wraps himself around me, protecting me from the world. The other arms want to leave me, but I grip them as tightly as I can.

"Don't worry, I won't leave you," they whisper - he whispers. Luther.

"Are you sure this is wise? Us being so close to her after all that just happened?" Ben is trying to be sensible, but he's hugging me to his chest, and I know he won't let go.

"She wants us here, she will tell us if she wants us to let go of her," Luther says and I want to agree, but it's hard to form a coherent sentence.

"Charlie is on her way," Alistair says from around the corner. "She'll be able to look at your arm as well, Ben."

That shocks me out of my delirium. Ben is hurt. I sit up, looking at him in panic. Ben can't be hurt.

"It's okay, it's just a scratch," he whispers reassuringly. "Relax, it will be fine."

"Did they...?" Alistair's voice is cold, precise.

"I don't think so," Luther replies quietly. "She was still tied to the chair when I arrived."

Al sighs. "We should have known. It was too easy. She shouldn't have been here alone. It's our fault."

"We know," Ben snarls and I shiver at his angry words. "Shh," he whispers immediately, giving me a reassuring squeeze. "I'm sorry, I'm not angry at you or Alistair. I'm just..." He shrugs helplessly, mirroring Al.

Al, who's still standing apart from us. I need him. He needs to be here.

I open my mouth, trying to form words, but all that comes out is a weak moan. Pain is clouding my mind. Just like before...

...can't breathe...

...him...

...no air...

"Breathe, Em!" Alistair's clear voice is suddenly close, commanding me to do as he says. "You need to breathe. You're safe. We're here."

He puts an arm around my shoulders, joining the others in our tangle of pain.

They're taking away some of the agony in my mind and body, just by being here. They ground me in the present, Al reminding me to breathe again and again, until Charlie arrives and gives me something for the pain, so I can sleep and forget.

♥

The boys take turns in putting cold bandages on my face. They make me sit up and drink, and check if I'm okay. I might have a concussion, Charlie said, and I need to have a proper examination tomorrow. She gave them some pain meds to give to me, but it hurts even with them. The pain in my mind is worse than the pain in my body though. When Ben comes with new wet cloths again, I make him join me on the bed until he hugs me tight, giving me a semblance of safety. He is warm and he shot them all.

He will protect me.

♥

I'm huddled between Ben and Alistair in the backseat of a cab, gripping their hands tightly. I've never been someone who gets easily scared but, right now, my body is in panic mode. And all we're doing is taking a taxi to a hotel. Not exactly a dangerous mission.

The living room is full of blood stains and bullet holes and bad memories, so we've decided to stay at a hotel for now. The only reason we've waited until now is that they wanted to give me some rest. Luther has driven ahead to arrange it all, and now we're following. The painkillers are wearing off, but I've refused to take any more. I want my head to be clear, even though my face and stomach hurt like hell. Both the paramedics and the guys wanted to take me to the hospital, but I refused. I've had enough of hospitals for a lifetime. I'm okay to go there for a check up tomorrow, and to have my cast x-rayed, but for now, I want to stay with my men. My subconscious seems to have decided that the guys are safe, and that I am safe wherever they are. Looking at what happened yesterday, that doesn't seem very rational, but emotional me doesn't care. All I want is Ben, Alistair and Luther.

The cab pulls over in front of a large, sparkly hotel and Ben helps me out, passing me my crutches. They wanted to take the wheelchair but I refused. I think I blame that thing for giving me away to those monsters.

I've got a baseball cap pulled deep over my face to hide the bruises. I don't want anyone to think that the guys did this to me. I know they're blaming themselves, and at some point, we need to address that. It's silly for them to feel guilty. Nobody knew this would be a trap.

Ben shot all five of them, two fatally. There's going to be an enquiry, but for now, he's allowed to stay with us. Guess he didn't lie when he told me about having a gun license when we first met. The others are in hospital under police supervision, and will be taken into custody as soon as they're well enough. Hopefully, the guys will be able to get information from them, not just about how they managed to fool us all, but also about who else is involved. And where they keep all those poor girls.

Thinking of them, my bruises hurt less. I was lucky, the guys came back just in time. Those girls have nobody coming to rescue them. Not until we have more intel, but a SOCA team is working on it while my men are taking care of me.

Luther awaits us in the lobby and leads us to a pretentious golden elevator. Our suite is on the top floor - and once again, I'm amazed at what the guys are able to afford. This isn't a simple set of rooms, this is a gigantic flat with several bedrooms, a fully equipped kitchen and two bathrooms. And a jacuzzi in the middle of one of them.

Luther catches me staring at it. "Would you like a bath?"

"I'd like nothing more," I say, trying to smile but failing utterly. I'm not quite there yet.

"I'll get it ready, just sit down and relax a bit."

"Wait... what about my leg?"

He grins and holds up a garish blue... thing. "Got that from the pharmacy around the corner. They say it is completely waterproof, even when taking a long bath." He unfolds the protective sleeve to unroll a thick, leg-shaped rubber bag. My heart melts at his thoughtfulness.

"Now, sit down, I won't be long."

I do as he asks, gingerly sitting down on the white stretched linen on one of the big four poster beds. I feel dirty, and not deserving of such cleanliness.

Someone knocks on the door and I freeze, panic setting in.

"Room service!"

Looking less cautious than I think he should be, Ben

opens the door and takes something from the man outside. He turns around with a smile.

"Hot chocolate, Em?"

This time I manage to smile. "You don't know how amazing you are."

"I don't?" He shoots me a toothy grin. "I could show you exactly how amazing I am."

"Are you flirting with me?"

He immediately turns serious. "I'm sorry, I shouldn't. Not after... everything."

I smile sadly. "Flirting is good. It's normal. I need normality right now."

"Well, then I'm going to try my very best to do some proper flirting."

"Ignore him, I'm the king of flirtiness," Alistair interrupts. "Did you know you make me melt just like that hot chocolate?" He grins foolishly as Ben breaks out in laughter.

"That was terrible. Try this one: You're even sweeter than hot chocolate."

I snort. "Sorry boys, but you really need to work on your pick-up lines."

"You're so hot, you should get into the jacuzzi before you burn the place," Luther smirks as he comes out of the bathroom, holding a towel and the cast protector. He gives me a bow. "My lady, your bath has been prepared."

"I don't deserve you guys," I mutter, tears welling up in my eyes. But maybe that's just from the delicious steam of the mug of cocoa in my hands.

"We don't deserve you," Ben whispers and gives me a gentle kiss on my forehead.

"Now get into that bath before the water gets cold," Luther says playfully and takes my mug from me. I growl and he laughs. "You'll get it back once you're lounging in the water."

"Does that mean you're going to come in when I'm naked?"

He pauses for a moment and I see the indecision behind his eyes. He's scared of how I will react. But I will make sure that this *thing* isn't going to come between us.

"If you would like me to?"

I smile at him. "You are very welcome to join me."

Alistair gasps in mock horror. "Now I'm offended. He gets to play with you and I'm not invited?"

I pretend to think hard. "I guess... if there's enough space... it wouldn't be fair if only one of you was in the bathtub with me."

With a wide grin, Luther kneels in front of me and pulls the blue waterproof bag over my cast. It looks hideous, but it's snug against my skin, hopefully not letting any water in. I should probably keep this bath quite short. If the cast gets wet, I might have to get a new one.

"Arms up," Alistair whispers, suddenly by my side. He takes off my shirt, letting it fall carelessly onto the floor. Ben climbs onto the bed and unclasps my bra from behind, gently running his hands over my skin.

"Is this okay?" he murmurs and presses a soft kiss on my shoulder blade.

"Yes. Make me forget," I sigh as he puts his hands on my breasts while Alistair leans forward to kiss my lips.

"Guys, the water is getting cold," Luther complains. "Get up, Em, before those two eat you alive."

That sounds like a promise that I would love them to keep, but I accept that cold bath water is a terrible thing. He hoists me up and I let him pull down my baggy joggers. Looking up with a cheeky smile, he takes the rim of my panties between his teeth and yanks them down. Cool air strokes my core and I shiver in pleasure.

The jacuzzi awaits.

# Sixteen

Luther carries me into the bathroom, with the other two following, already half naked. Ben has a bandage around his left bicep, but I can't see this preventing him from joining us in the bath.

My bare skin is rubbing against Luther's shirt, giving me goosebumps. I want him, I want them all. Why am I so horny? I should be exhausted, traumatised, depressed, but instead, I want them to fuck me. I'm so messed up.

Candles are flickering all around the room, smelling of cinnamon and pine needles. Luther hands me to Alistair while he slips out of his clothes, but immediately takes me back when he's naked. I snuggle against his hot skin, savouring the touch.

Luther gently lowers me into the water - just the right temperature, hot, but not scalding - while Alistair holds up my broken leg, seemingly forgetting that the sleeve is supposed to protect it. Ben just stands there and grins like he won a prize at the carnival. Am I the prize? Or is he mine?

When we're fully submerged in the water, Luther doesn't let go of me like I thought he would. No, he keeps his arms wrapped around my belly, holding me tight.

"I was so worried," he whispers so only I can hear. "I thought I wouldn't be able to see you again, hold you again. Never talk to you, hug you, sleep with you, tell you... Emily. You've brought so much drama into our life, but it's totally worth it. And I think-"

A splash stops him as Ben jumps into the jacuzzi with a laugh.

He grins at us. "Interrupting something?"

Luther grumbles under his breath but doesn't respond.

Ben chuckles and turns on the bubbles.

Thousands of tiny tickles run over my skin. My brain can't cope with it. I moan.

"We haven't even started yet," Alistair says softly, wrapping his hands through my hair and pulling my head back until I'm leaning against the rim of the basin, looking up at his beautiful eyes. He's kneeling on the floor, naked, aroused. Beautiful.

He kisses me, his nose touching my skin, his neck rubbing against my sore cheeks. I'm just glad that the guys are ignoring the purple bruises forming on my skin. I couldn't deal with looks of pity just now.

I can feel the stubble waiting to turn into a beard, and I wonder what he would look like with facial hair. With his white-blond hair, I imagine it would be stunning. I smile into our kiss and open my lips, letting him in. He sucks at my bottom lip, giving it a gentle bite.

My insides contract in pleasure and my legs open of their own volition. I am ready for them.

Luther is hard against my back and I begin to rub my bum against him, teasing, provoking. Ben is sitting on the other side of the jacuzzi, half hidden behind all the bubbles. He's got one hand on the edge, the other disappears underneath the surface. I imagine him rubbing himself and moan as I open up, water entering me. Luther starts to massage my breasts while Al's kiss is getting deeper. He's pushing his tongue down my throat, and I wish it was something else. I shift, breaking our kiss. He looks at me in confusion.

"Let me taste you," I whisper and his eyes light up. He sits down on the edge, legs hanging in the water, his cock erect and ready for me. I turn until I kneel on Luther's thighs - eliciting a groan from him - and hold onto his shoulders as I take Alistair's cock into my mouth. He is pulsating with lust, thick and satisfying. I swirl my tongue around his head before taking him all the way in, swallowing until he's close to my throat. He feels so good.

Alistair groans as I start to move my head up and down, sucking on him as hard as I can. Something presses against my entrance and I wiggle my bum in invitation. Ben enters me slowly, letting me adjust to his girth.

"Don't stop," Al commands hoarsely, and I continue sliding up and down his dick, gently grazing him with my teeth. He twitches and I know it's time to stop. I don't want him to come yet.

Suddenly, I feel in control. These three men are here for me, because of me, with me. And in Ben's case, in me.

He is moving leisurely in and out of me, letting me

experience each thrust in agonising slowness. I think he's convinced I'm breakable and that he needs to be careful. I don't want him to, I want him to fuck me properly, make me forget, take me to that special place where nothing but pleasure exists. I grind against him, trying to get the message across. I'm ready for more.

Luckily, Luther decides to take one of my nipples into his mouth. My breasts are just above the water's surface, and the bubbles tickle their undersides in the most delicious way. I arch my back, giving him more access.

With a splash, Alistair steps into the jacuzzi, his cock begging me to touch him. I put one hand around him, the other around Luther's, and begin to stroke them hard.

"Easy," Al yelps and teasingly pulls on my nipples in response.

"Tell Ben to do more," I grumble and they laugh.

Ben disappears from inside me and I worry I may have upset him, but then something presses against my arse. Oh. That's new. And exciting. And painful. And amazing.

Slowly, he widens me, entering that unfamiliar place. I moan and he chuckles, kissing the back of my neck.

"Is that better?" he asks teasingly and slides out, only to thrust in a second later. All I can do is nod.

Luther puts a hand between my legs, teasing me with the tips of his fingers.

"More," I groan and he slips a finger inside me. Usually, one finger isn't enough to make me satisfied, but with Ben fucking my arse, I'm filled to the brink. My moans are getting louder as they bring me to new heights.

I'm gripping Luther's shoulders, their cocks forgotten. My mind is busy trying not to explode.

Then Luther adds a second finger while his thumb presses on my bud - and I'm in heaven, coming, floating. I scream in ecstasy while I feel Ben come in my arse. But there is no rest for the wicked. Luther continues to fuck me with his fingers, adding a third. Alistair wades through the water until he's behind me, taking Ben's place, easily slipping into me.

"Are you ready for two of us?" Luther whispers, his fingers leaving me with a promise of more.

"Take me," I moan, quivering with each of Al's strong thrusts. He grips my hips and pulls me close, giving him even deeper access. It won't take long to bring me over the edge again. Luther lifts me and spreads my legs until I'm positioned right over his hard cock.

"Ready?" he asks and, without waiting for confirmation, pulls me down until I sit on him, both of their cocks deeply imbedded within me. I cry out in pleasure as I can feel them touch each other through my inner walls. So close, so much, so full. I whimper as Alistair starts to move. He's taking it slow and this time, I'm actually grateful for it. I've never felt so full before, but it's amazing, despite the pain.

Ben takes my chin with his scarred hand and moves me towards his cock. I didn't even notice he had left the jacuzzi and is now sitting where Al was before, ready for me to take him into my mouth. He's hard again. I gently lick him from the bottom to the top, eliciting a groan.

The guys' pace is getting faster, and with each thrust, my breasts are slapping against the water's surface, electricity running through my nipples and down into my core. I can feel my muscles tightening in anticipation.

"Relax," Luther whispers and gently strokes my wet hair out of my face. "Just let go. We've got you."

They both pull out, leaving two empty spaces inside of me. I want to protest, but then they're back, both at the same time, filling me completely. I explode and, this time, I don't hold back. I scream as I ride the endless waves of pleasure racing through my body. They continue to fuck me, hard and fast, but I am in another sphere, removed from my body, blinking into the lights that surround me.

This is where I want to be. My three men inside me, whispering words of love, making me whole.

# Seventeen



Mary puts a large piece of carrot cake in front of me, next to the half-empty mug of cocoa and the slightly stained letter I've been staring at for the past five minutes.

Turns out, I'm rich. The zeros are dancing in front of my eyes. So much money. Compensation for the 'trouble' I went through two weeks ago, plus my first salary. We're here to celebrate, in the place Ben took me to when we first met. The hot chocolate is just as good as I remember.

"Em, I'd like you to meet our boss," Alistair says suddenly and waves Mary over, the café's owner.

"Wait, what?"

Mary smiles and takes a seat on the fifth chair that the guys have left empty.

"Hello again," she says with a wide grin. "I'm M, and yes, the letter M, just like in James Bond. It's short for Mary but it's more fun to have a proper code name."

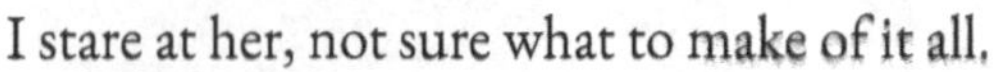

I stare at her, not sure what to make of it all.

"But you're..."

"Working in a café?" she completes my sentence. "Yes, sweetie, that's my hobby. It's very handy for operatives working undercover. They come here, have a scone, while giving me information to pass on."

I think back to the first time we came here.

"So when Ben took me here at the beginning... it wasn't just because this is a nice café?"

Ben chuckles. "No, she wanted to check you out. M's our superior and we needed her approval to employ you. You were classed as a vulnerable adult, living on the streets, so M had to make sure we're not taking advantage of your circumstances."

"You made it pretty clear that you can look after yourself," Mary says with a smile. Her eyes flicker to the chocolaty fingerprints on the white paper. "And now that you're part of us, you can come here whenever you need advice. Or a hot chocolate."

I look at the numbers again. So much money. This means I'll never have to return to the streets. I'm independent now, I'll no longer have to rely on the guys. I can even pay them back for all the clothes and gadgets they bought me. Although Ben would probably spank my arse for that. He's been doing that a lot recently. He's turned out a lot more dominant than I expected. And I absolutely love it.

"Is there something wrong with the cake?" Mary asks with a cheeky grin. "Do you want some more cream?"

"No, but some champagne would be nice. I'm buying," I reply while signing at the bottom of the letter, finishing with a flourish, confirming that I'm accepting both the compensation and my new contract of employment.

She chuckles. "I'm not strictly speaking licensed to sell alcohol, but I believe your boys took care of that."

Ben frowns at her calling them 'boys', but he takes a bottle of bubbly out of his backpack. Mary provides the glasses and joins us at the small table.

She holds up her glass, smiling at me.

"Welcome to SOCA."

It's a strange feeling to clink glasses with her. This old lady? The guys' boss? Seriously? She seems too sweet to be a spy, but I guess that's exactly why she's good at it.

Mary turns to the guys. "Have you heard the news yet? The trafficking ring has been shut down and the girls are being looked after by social services."

"Who caught them?" Alistair asks excitedly.

"Tamal and his team. They took over where you boys left off after the *incident*. Turns out these men weren't just involved in human trafficking but also groomed local girls."

"Did they find out how they got our address?"

She grimaces. "They knew they were being watched, so they put a tracker on your car while you were sneaking around. I assume it was a few days before the actual incident. They wanted you out of the house so they could find out who you were and what you wanted. How much of a threat you were, before they confronted you openly. Emily being there was just an unlucky coincidence. I don't think they knew she was living with you."

I swallow hard. Well, that's me, unlucky. Somehow, I

keep getting into situations where people attack me. At least once I get rid of my cast, I can defend myself better. Alistair is going to help me with learning new self-defence moves once I've got my full movement back. If I'm going to be a valued part of their team, I can't be reliant on them to protect me.

"Ben, we've got a hearing set for Monday, then you should get your weapon back. You know how it is, it takes time for reports to filter through the various inboxes."

He sighs. "Last time it only took a few days, not two weeks."

Mary smiles. "I thought you deserved a holiday."

Ben stares at her for a moment, then smiles back.

"Thanks. It was good to be able to spend some time with Em while she recovers."

He's right about that. Last week, we moved back to the house after spending a week at the hotel.. The living room has been completely redone and while it looks very different from before, I'm glad there are no traces of the blood stains left. Alistair has installed a new security system that requires a fingerprint to open the front door. Of course people could still break in by demolishing the door itself, but at least nobody will be able to pick the lock. The windows are all alarmed now too. Before, even though they all work in a dangerous field, the men didn't seem to worry about their safety at home. Now, that's changed though. I don't know if it's just because of me or because they were affected by the invasion of their home, their safe space; but the entire house is now full of sensors and alarms.

"When you come for your hearing, bring Emily, she

might want to meet some of the others," Mary says, pulling me from my thoughts. "I think your colleagues are all rather curious about her."

"They can stay curious," Luther mutters, annoyance lacing his tone. "She's ours. They can find their own Em."

Mary laughs. "For now, she's in your team, but as long as I'm paying her, I reserve the right to assign her to other teams if necessary." She turns to me. "And if you ever want to split from the boys, just let me know. Your job isn't linked to them. Don't be afraid that you could lose your income if you want to be apart from them."

I nod, although I don't have any intentions of being apart from my guys ever again. They're mine. Charlie visited several times during the past two weeks, mainly to check on me, but I've been trying to keep her visits short. I never knew my jealous streak was so intense, but these men bring out both the best and the worst in me.

# Eighteen

I've got a new task but, for the first time, I'm not as excited about it as I should be. It's not hard to find the reason for that: Alistair is sprawled out on the sofa, his shirt ruffled up, exposing part of his flat stomach. He's just come home from work and looks exhausted, but also very delicious. I'd love to go over to him and kiss that small streak of exposed skin, but I know I should really be finishing this translation. It might be really important. It's something about money and loans and debt, nothing terribly exciting. But who knows what the backstory to this is? Where there's money, there's crime. Simple.

For now, the guys are banned from fieldwork. After the drama of their last mission, they're supposed to lie low and catch up on paperwork. They're not enjoying it. Strangely enough, Alistair is the one who has to go out the most now. Usually, he prefers to work from home, doing stuff on his computer, but there are meetings to attend in town, people to question, gadgets to approve. To have him here, in the same room, has become a rarity.

"Busy day?" I ask him and he groans in response.

"If I have to sit in one more boardroom and listen to some boring people talk about stuff they don't know anything about, I'm going to quit my job and go freelance."

"Would that be possible?"

He shrugs and turns onto his side, looking straight at me.

"There's always a demand for ex-intelligence agents, but despite what I say, I do love my job. Don't listen to me complain. Tell me what you're doing instead."

He gives me a smile that reaches all the way into my heart. Gone is the Alistair who sometimes looked at me as if he didn't quite want me here. He's all warmth and happiness now.

"Someone's borrowed money from several people and they are trying to get it back."

"Mafia?" he asks.

"No, it looks like a group of very wealthy Russians. They might be mafia, who knows? But on paper they just look like businessmen."

I sigh. "It's not the most exciting work ever."

Alistair grins. "I think you need a distraction."

I raise an eyebrow. "What are you thinking?" I'm hoping it has something to do with me taking off his clothes.

"I've not been to the zoo in ages," he says with a shrug. "And they've got a special event on tonight, just for adults. Visiting the zoo after their usual opening times, with cocktails, nibbles, and presentations about the animals. Want to go?"

That's so Alistair. He wants to go to the zoo. I would never have thought of doing that, never in a million years, but it does sound like fun. Maybe not the presentations, but I love a good cocktail.

There's only one problem...

"I don't think I can walk through the entire zoo," I tell him, remembering how Edinburgh zoo is built on a steep slope. "And I really don't want to sit in a wheelchair again."

He frowns, then takes out his phone and starts to type. A moment later, his expression lightens again.

"They've got a little electric mobility vehicle that we can use." He gives me a wink. "Tonight, we'll travel in style."

I can't help but imagine one of those mobility scooters that old people often use, but hopefully that's not what he's talking about. I don't want to stand out, I don't want people to stare. I've had far too much attention recently and I can really do without it.

"Okay, let's do this."

He smiles widely and immediately jumps off the sofa, no longer looking tired in the slightest. "I'll tell the others. You might want to put on some warmer clothes though, it's going to be cold."


Two hours later, we arrive at the zoo. It must be at least ten years since I've last been here, but not much seems to have changed. A row of steps leads up to a large pavilion which houses the ticket office and a shop. I remember begging my parents to buy me some kind of plush animal from the shop, but they never did. Maybe I can get one today. It's not like I'm poor. I still can't believe my bank balance. It's crazy, and in a way, I hope that I'll never get used to it. I don't want to become spoiled or used to luxury. I want to stay me, Em, someone who's worked all her life to get to where she is now.

At the bottom of the steps, a zoo employee is waiting for us in front of a brightly painted golf buggy, the kind rich people drive on golf courses. Is that the mobility vehicle? I can't help but grin. This really is going to be fun.

"Our chariot awaits," Ben snickers and opens the car door for me, helping me out. That's something that's not easy to do with crutches and I'm grateful for his help.

While Luther drives away to park the car, we head towards the buggy.

"Miss Malone?" the man asks, smiling at me. He seems a little confused that I'm accompanied by two men though.

"Yes, that's me."

He points at the buggy. "Would you like me to drive or will one of your companions do so?"

Ben stretches out a hand, quietly demanding the keys. "I'll drive."

The man hands him the keys and with a few words about not going too fast and where to park it once we're done, he disappears.

"I've always wanted to drive one of these," Ben laughs. "May I be your designated driver for tonight?"

Alistair looks like he's about to protest, but then lets

Ben take the driver seat. He helps me on the seat besides Ben, taking my crutches and putting them in the back.

"Are you warm enough?" he asks and I nod.

"I'm cold, thanks for asking," Ben says. "I'm looking forward to some mulled wine."

Luther slides into the back row of the buggy. I hadn't even realised he was back.

"So, what are we going to look at first?" he asks excitedly. "I love the rhinos."

"Penguins," Alistair says, as if the thought of going to see rhinos personally offended him.

Ben chuckles. "One of the pandas is supposed to be pregnant."

Suddenly, they all look at me.

"Ehm... are there any tigers?"

They stare, then they laugh.

"Tigers it is," Ben says and starts the buggy's engine. It's an electric vehicle, so it's almost inaudible.

We drive towards the main gate which gets opened as soon as we approach.

"Don't we have to buy tickets?" I ask as we pass through the gate without being stopped.

Alistair wiggles his phone in front of me. "Already done. We've got the VIP tickets, so all the food and drinks are included."

"Great job," Luther says, patting Alistair on the back. It sounds as if it would hurt. Luther is not a small guy, nor is he particularly gentle. Except with me. I smile. He can be very gentle sometimes.

Night has fallen, but the zoo is illuminated brightly. Lampions are hanging from the trees and fairy lights are covering the bushes lining the paths. Still, it's hard to make out what the signs say, so Alistair pulls out his phone again and downloads a map of the zoo. There are people everywhere, but they make way for the buggy without Ben having to use the horn. It's strange to see the zoo at night, and even stranger not to have any children running around.

When we make it to the big cat enclosure, rows and rows of tiny stalls await us.

"Tigers first or a drink first?" Ben asks.

"Drink," the guys in the back say as one, so I shrug and let Ben drive us to a wooden hut where they sell a variety of hot drinks. Including amaretto hot chocolate.

"That one!" I say, pointing at the sign.

Luther roars in laughter, making everyone stare at him. "Of course, little chocolate addict."

"I'm neither little nor an addict," I complain, but he's already out of the buggy to order our drinks.


The alcohol is making me feel warm and comfy. As we drive through the zoo, I snuggle against Ben while Alistair massages my shoulders from behind. The tigers were asleep despite the crowds surrounding their enclosure, but we get to see a host of other animals, including Luther's beloved rhinos. The giant pandas are out of bounds because of the possibility of the female being pregnant, so we end up looking at the red pandas instead. There are two of them, a male and a female, but they're separated by a metal fence.

Luther gets out to read the sign.

"They're being kept apart until they get to know each other better," he says once he's returned to the buggy.

"What if they don't like each other?" I ask. "Will they have to stay together?"

"No idea. Your guess is as good as mine. I would hope not, but maybe they are soulmates who've been waiting to be with each other all their life. Imagine how happy they'll be once that fence is removed."

Alistair laughs. "Are you turning into a big old romantic, Lou?"

"I've always been a romantic," Luther says calmly. "But maybe I just hadn't found the person to show it to yet."

He taps me on my shoulder until I turn around.

"I think I've found her now."

He smiles and bends forward to kiss me. It's an awkward angle, but I twist until our mouths meet. This time, his kiss is soft and gentle, as if he wants to prove how romantic he is. I'll have to tell him later that romance isn't all about everything being soft and sweet. There can be a whole lot of other, spicier layers.

His tongue nudges my lips until I open my mouth a little. I let him in, meeting his tongue with my own. He leans forward, closing the last tiny space between us.

"Get a room," Alistair mutters but he doesn't stop us. He probably banks on our little pact: what I do with one of them, I'll also do with the other two. It's a simple enough rule, one I'm happy to follow. We don't want there to be any imbalance in our relationship.

From the corner of my eye, I see Alistair getting out of the buggy, but I ignore him and focus on kissing

Luther - until he suddenly wraps his arms around my waist.

"Ey, I'm busy!" I complain as he lifts me up and pulls me out of the buggy.

"I know," he whispers in my ear. "I want you to be even busier."

He carries me to the back of the buggy and sits me down on the bench next to Luther, before sliding in next to me. I'm sandwiched between the two men, and because the bench isn't very wide, it's a rather tight squeeze.

"What are you doing?" Ben asks, still in the driver's seat.

"Getting a room," Alistair mutters and pulls a blanket from his backpack. He throws it over our laps, but I don't think he's doing it because he's cold. He grins at me and then takes my right hand, guiding it towards his blanket-covered crotch. What a devious, devious man.

Not that I'm complaining. Making sure that the blanket is really hiding what I'm about to do, I stroke my hand up and down, feeling him harden beneath the fabric of his jeans. I look over at Luther, who's watching us with a longing expression. I smile and slip my left hand under the blanket, feeling for his cock. He's hard already.

"Are you doing what I think you're doing?" Ben asks, looking at us with a smirk. "It's a pity you don't have three hands, Em."

I feel the same regret. "Later," I promise. "You'll get the same later."

Alistair groans and, after a quick look in case anyone's watching, opens his zipper, letting his cock jump free, right into my hand. He's not wearing any underwear. Why am I not surprised?

Luther does the same and suddenly, I have two cocks in my hands, hard and twitching, waiting for me to bring them over the edge.

"And what about me?" I ask with a smirk. "Is this going to be one sided?"

Luther moves his lips to my ear and whispers, "Whatever you do to us now, I'll do to you twofold when we're back home."

My belly tightens at his words and I feel the heat pool between my legs. Well, that's a promise I'm going to hold him to.

I glide my hands along both of their cocks, applying just a tiny bit of pressure, just enough to make them breathe a little faster. Ben has turned around and is watching us intently, not saying anything, his eyes locking with mine. I smile and begin to rub their cocks harder, hoping that he knows what I'm doing to his friends. Maybe, in some strange way, he can feel it too.

"More," Alistair groans, but I don't increase my pace, not yet. I continue to look into Ben's eyes, not changing my rhythm. His gaze is mesmerising, I'm falling into him and he's embracing me inside, wrapping me up warm and guiding me back to the surface. He's my good samaritan, the man who picked me up and then helped me stand by myself again.

I swirl my index fingers over the silky tips of their cocks, eliciting more groans and loud breaths. I smile and begin to fuck them in earnest, my hands pumping them, up and down, my fingers squeezing in all the right places.

Luther is the first to twitch, then he comes with a suppressed roar, his hand landing on my thigh and squeezing hard as the orgasm rips through him. Alistair follows shortly after, but still Ben is looking at me with a small smirk. I want to kiss him, kiss them all, make love to them here and now. I've never felt such a bond to anyone, but here I am, surrounded by three men, all of them perfect and unique, as if they were made to fill the empty spaces within me.

We leave pretty quickly after that, none of us having the patience to spend more time at the zoo when there's something much more feral we could do. Ben carries me into the house, my crutches still in the car. He drops me on the sofa then stands up tall, looking down at me.

"My turn," he says hoarsely and unzips his trousers, stepping out of them and carelessly throwing them onto the ground. He's hard and erect, and probably has been for a while. The other two have joined us in the living room, but they simply sit down on the two armchairs on the other side of the room and watch. Now, it's time to make Ben happy, those two have already had their treat.

I beckon him closer and he steps forward until his cock is at the same level as my mouth. Very handy. Keeping my hands in my lap, I kiss him, and as soon as my lips touch him, Ben groans and jerks his hips, his cock slapping against my cheek. I take that as encouragement and take him into my mouth, lapping up his taste. He's so familiar by now. He's mine.

I glide my lips along his smooth, hard skin until I can't take him any further.

"Look at me," he demands and I do as he says, meeting his eyes. "Don't look away," he warns with an intensity that makes me shiver.

"Dominant Ben has come out to play," Luther whispers to Alistair in the background, and I know exactly what they mean. This is Ben the interrogator, the man who won't take no for an answer, the man who will push me to my limits and beyond. But he's also Ben the lover, who would do anything for me, who will bring me the pleasure I crave.

Not lowering my gaze, I retreat until he's only just about touching my lips, before taking him back into my mouth, sucking him, applying pressure with my lips. Again, he jerks his hips, probably involuntarily. He plays with my hair while I suck him off, massaging my scalp with the tips of his fingers. It's a strangely innocent gesture compared to what I'm doing to him.

His eyes keep mine trapped, even when his cheeks fill with colour and his breath grows louder. Even when he comes in my mouth, he's looking at me, never wavering, telling me that he'll always be there for me.

# Nineteen

I wake with a strange feeling. Maybe I had a bad dream, maybe it's remnants of memories that haunted my subconsciousness while I slept, but for some reason, I'm scared. Not of anything in particular, just... scared.

I look around. Nobody there, it's just me. I grab my phone from the nightstand and check the time. 8:21. I think we were up until four in the morning, the guys returning the attention I had shown them before. It had been a good night. I try to smile but I can't bring myself to be happy.

There are three unread messages.

Genius: *Morning, we were called into the office, emergency meeting.*

Gladiator: *Morning, how did you sleep? I had fun last night. Didn't have time to make breakfast, but I'll make up for it later.*

Superman: *You snored. Love you nonetheless.*

Again, the smile dies before it reaches my lips. Something's wrong.

I get up and take my crutches. After last night, I'd love to have a shower now, but I can't do that without help yet. The one time I tried, I almost broke even more bones. Once the guys are back, I'm going to ask one of them to help me. Much better than that nurse. I shudder at the memory.

Just like every morning, I head to the kitchen. There's a white envelope on the counter with neither a name nor address on it. Did the guys leave that here for me? A surprise, maybe? If it was a secret not intended for my eyes, they wouldn't have left it leaning against the sugar bowl.

I take the envelope and carefully open it. Inside is a folded piece of paper.

The three sentences on it are in Albanian.

*You took what was mine.*

*Now I've taken what was yours.*

*She died alone.*

A cold feeling spreads through my stomach and I grip the edges of the counter, unsure of what I just read. This is bad. It's not a message from the guys, it's directed at them. And it's not a friendly one at that. I search my dressing gown pockets for my phone, but I must have left it in the bedroom. Fuck.

I put the letter in my pocket, so I have my hands free for the crutches, then hop back as fast as I can. I need to tell them. Someone's in danger. A thought that I've pushed away until now barges its way to the forefront of my mind. They were in the house. The letter was placed there not by the guys, but by someone else. It must have happened this morning, while I was sleeping. They would have noticed when they had their breakfast.

When I reach the bedroom, my phone isn't on the nightstand. Nor is it on the bed. Nor under it. Nor anywhere else in the room. Fuck. Where did I put it? It must be somewhere.

I check my pockets. Nothing.

I swear it was here before I went to the kitchen and I didn't take it with me. I can no longer hold back the fear that is threatening to overwhelm me.

I hop back to the kitchen, cursing the crutches that prevent me from running. No phone on the counter. Do the guys have a landline? I've never seen one in the house, but maybe there's one in Alistair's office. Otherwise, I can send them an email from there, maybe I'll be lucky and they'll see it quickly. Before something happens.

I have a very bad feeling about this. I turn - and shriek when I see the paint on the wall beside the kitchen door. It's red, dripping onto the floor, freshly brushed onto the wall.

**HELP**

This wasn't here two minutes ago.

My heart begins to beat even harder, my breath quick and shallow. They're in the house, right now, with me. They're toying with me.

I need to get to the office.

I grip my crutches tighter and leave the kitchen as fast as I can. As I pass the door, a drop of paint drips onto my cheek. I wipe it off, my fingers stained red. Someone is playing a game that I'm refusing to play. This house is my home and they're not going to take that away from me.

"Come and show yourself!" I shout, anger driving the fear away. "Stop hiding!"

Nothing happens. I can't hear anyone move, but I didn't before and they were clearly here. Hell, they painted the kitchen. If that isn't a clear calling mark, then I don't know what is.

"I'm waiting!" I shout loudly, sounding far more confident than I am.

Still, nothing.

Okay then, back to my original plan. Problem is, Alistair's office is on the first floor. I'm used to climbing stairs with my crutches by now, but it's slow and will make me even more vulnerable than I am here on solid ground. Why don't they have a landline somewhere in the hallway or living room, where normal people have one? As much as I like having a mobile phone, right now, I don't like the trend of using that for everything.

Suddenly, there's a sound from above, like something fell onto the floor. Most of the rooms upstairs are carpeted, but this didn't sound muffled enough. No, this has to be in the bathroom, and judging from how close above me it was, it must be Luther's bathroom.

Okay, now I know where they are, but that doesn't help me in the slightest. It's not like I can go up there and confront them. I don't have any weapons, I can't defend myself properly. No, the only thing I can do is run.

I turn and head for the main door at the end of the hallway, away from the staircase leading up. Please let them be slow. Please let them stay in the bathroom and not follow me.

I press down the door handle - and it's locked. I pull and pull, but it's deadlocked. The fingerprint sensor is only on the outside; in here, it's an old-fashioned handle. How the fuck did they manage to lock it? It should only be locked for people wanting to get in, not the other way round.

I want to kick the door in frustration, but I manage to restrain myself. Let's think. There's an intruder, I can't get out of the door, I can't fight, I don't have a phone.

Windows. The ones in the living room are the biggest, so I limp there, my arms beginning to hurt from gripping the crutches so tightly.

As soon as I enter the living room, I stop in my tracks. I want to cry. There's more paint, this time on the windows, a smiley face, staring at me, mocking me. I bet they've locked the windows too. Oh well, guess I'll have to resort to violence.

I close the living room door behind me and push one of the armchairs underneath the door handle, hoping that will stop the intruder from following me in here, at least for a bit. I can do this, I can get out of this without being assaulted, kidnapped or killed. I'm not going to be a victim for the third time. I'm going to prove to myself and to the guys that I'm strong.

Not a victim.

I search the room for something to break the window with. The armchairs are too heavy to lift, but there's a poker by the fireplace. I think it's just decoration, but it's heavy and iron, so that should hopefully work. Otherwise, I'll have my crutches to try with.

There are no sounds coming from upstairs, nobody trying to break into the room. I don't have time to think about what they're doing, or what this is all about. I need to get out of here.

I lift the poker like a baseball bat and smash it against the window as hard as I can.

The window doesn't shatter like I had hoped, but there's a small crack in the centre of it. I can work with that. I hit the glass again and, this time, the cracks lengthen, almost reaching the edges of the window. One more smash with the poker and the window shatters, tiny pieces of glass flying into my face, raining down on the floor. There's a noise up above me, but I don't stay to find out what it was. I use my crutches to remove the ragged shards from the window edges, then climb out as fast as I can. I'm only wearing a dressing gown, not the best attire for a daring escape.

My legs scrape against the remains of the glass, but the pain doesn't fully register in my brain. I'm too focused on escaping.

As soon as I've got both feet on the grass outside, I run as fast as I can, using my crutches to swing myself forward, faster than I've ever done so before. Alistair's house is at the end of a long driveway, but there are neighbouring houses at the end of it, I just need to get there. It's only a hundred yards or so. I can do this.

"Run, little girl, run!" a gravelly voice suddenly shouts from behind me. Despite my fears, I turn around. A man, his face covered by a large hood, is looking down at me from the first floor window. He doesn't seem like he's in a hurry to catch me. Why isn't he coming after me?

"This is making it so much more exciting!" he calls out, laughing. "Run!"

Okay, it's really beginning to get creepy, but I follow his advice and run as fast as my crutches allow. Not much further. I can already see one of the houses in the distance. I'll be safe soon. They'll be able to call the police and the guys will come. Nobody is going to hurt me, not ever again. I'm not letting them.

I turn my head every few steps, but he's not following me. He's disappeared from the window, maybe he's coming, maybe he's on the way. I need to be faster.

When I reach the first house, my arms and legs are hurting and I'm struggling to breathe. I frantically hit the door knocker, leaning against the wall to steady myself. Please let someone be in. Please.

There are footsteps coming closer, inside, and my heart begins to calm a little, just a tiny bit. Hope.

A woman opens the door, her hair tousled as if she's only just woken up.

"Help," I gasp. "Police."

She stares at me in shock, but then turns and holds the door open for me. I follow her inside and she shuts the door, locking it.

"What's going on?" she asks, her voice quivering.

"Do you have a phone?" I ask and she nods, handing me a sleek mobile phone.

I dial Alistair's number. He made me memorise it and now I'm incredibly grateful that he did.

He answers immediately.

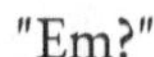

"Em?"

"There was someone in the house," I wheeze. "They took my phone, locked the door. I broke a window, I'm with a neighbour."

I'm not sure I'm making much sense but Alistair seems to understand.

"Did they follow you?"

"I don't think so. He told me to run."

He's quiet for a moment, then he shouts something, his voice muffled, he must be holding his hand against the microphone.

"We're on our way. Which neighbour are you with?"

"The first house, the one with the blue roof."

"Stay there, lock all doors and windows. Don't let anyone in until I tell you to. Stay on the phone."

"Okay."

My legs are struggling to keep me upright and I lean heavily against the wall. The woman has disappeared, hopefully to lock any other doors or windows that might be open.

"The police are coming as well. Are you hurt?"

"No, I don't think so."

"You don't think so?" His voice is sharp. Deadly.

I look at my legs. There's blood running down them from where I cut myself on the glass.

"Just a few scratches," I mutter.

"Do you need an ambulance?"

I weakly shake my head. "No, I'm fine. Just come here quickly."

"We're on our way," he repeats, grimly. There are

noises in the background, voices shouting. I hope the others are with him. "How many people were there?"

The woman is back, handing me a glass of water. I take it, noticing how my hands are shaking. I take a long sip, then hand the glass back to the woman.

"There's a basement," she says. "We can hide there."

I'm surprised at how well she's taking it all. She's asked almost no questions and doesn't seem to be scared by the prospect of someone trying to get into her house.

I nod and she leads the way, down the hallway and then through a narrow staircase leading into a musty smelling basement.

"Em, are you still there?" Alistair asks, almost shouting.

"Yes, we're in the basement now," I explain, leaning against a wall while the woman shuts the door. There's only a small, weak lamp illuminating the room, but there's not much to see anyway. A few crates in the corner, some pipes on the walls.

"Good. Stay there," he orders. "How many people?"

I notice I haven't answered his question yet. "I only saw the one, and only when I was already out of the house. They... there was paint..."

My voice breaks.

"Concentrate," Alistair orders, his voice calm. "Tell me everything from the beginning."

I do as he asks. When I mention the letter, he curses, but doesn't interrupt me. The woman has sat down on the floor and is watching me curiously. She's not said anything, nor asked any questions. Strange.

"And then?" Alistair asks. Oh. I've stopped talking.

"I..."

There's a loud knock on the door above us.

"Are you there yet?" I ask quickly. "Someone's here."

"No, let me check if it's the police." He goes quiet for a moment. "Yes, you can open the door, it's them. Stay in the house though, we'll be there in a few minutes."

I tell the woman and she gets up, leaving the basement while I stay here. I sink down to the floor, relief flooding me. I'm safe now. The guys aren't here yet, but the police are. The intruder won't be able to get me.

My breathing is slowly getting back to normal. No, actually, it's getting slower. Very slow.

"Alistair," I wheeze, my hands shaking even more than they did a moment ago. "Something's wrong."

"What do you mean?" he asks sharply. "We're almost there."

A strange sensation rolls over my body. A tingling, like water is being poured over me, then my arms go slack and the phone drops to the floor. I'm having trouble keeping my head upright. My lungs hurt, breathing is getting painful. What's going on? My fingers are itching and I want to move them, but I can't.

"Al..." my voice breaks before I can even say his name. My head falls to my chest and I slump forward, unable to stop myself.

Alistair is speaking, shouting even, but the phone is too far away for me to understand him.

I try to speak, tell him that I can't move, but my mouth won't cooperate. Everything is heavy, even my eyelids. The tingles have started to hurt, but it's not proper pain yet. I can handle this. In a moment, everything will be fine.

I feel drool running from my open mouth and I'm unable to stop it. I can't even close my lips. I'm completely paralysed, not a single muscle working. Wait, my heart's still working. So are my lungs, even though breathing is really starting to hurt now.

Where has the woman gone? Where are my guys? I can't look around, but my ears are still working. There are voices up above, probably the police. I will them to come to me, to help me.

At least my mind is still functioning. I don't feel like I'm about to faint, so that's a plus. For once. Why does this stuff always happen to me? How can one person be so unlucky to be attacked three times within just a few weeks? If this was a film, I'd have switched off by now, thinking that it wasn't realistic enough. Yet here I am, paralysed, unable to call for help, completely reliant on someone to come and find me. Life sucks.

A sharp pain stings in my chest when I breathe in the next time. Not good. I can't even wince at the pain, nor can I cry.

Don't be a victim, Em.

Finally, someone's coming down the stairs.

"Oh no, you said she was fine."

An unfamiliar voice, a woman.

"She was when I left her." The neighbour is there as well. It's not her fault, she's right, I was fine when she went upstairs to open the door. But now I'm not fine.

Every breath makes a weird, scary sound. My brain

isn't getting enough oxygen and I'm feeling a little faint. I'd probably see black spots if my eyes weren't shut.

"Miss, can you hear me?" The woman is shaking my shoulders. Well, that's not going to help. It only makes my head even woozier.

"Get an ambulance!" she shouts, her voice shrill. "We've got a situation down here."

Yes, we do. I laugh inside my head. It's a very strange situation.

"SOCA is here!" someone shouts back from afar. My guys, finally.

It only takes a moment for them to surround me.

"Em? Can you hear me?"

Ben. He's touching my wrist, probably taking my pulse. Someone's lifting my eyelids. I look at Luther, his face so full of pain and concern that I want to reach out and hug him, but of course that's impossible.

"You said she was fine," he grunts accusingly, looking at Alistair.

"She was. This only just happened."

"Her pulse is too slow," Ben says. "He never touched her, right? He didn't give her anything?"

"No," Alistair confirms. "Maybe she drank something? Maybe it's some kind of poison?"

I feel like coughing, something's blocking my throat, but I can't cough it away. I really need them to do something, it's getting harder to hold on.

"Is she unconscious?" Alistair asks from somewhere above me.

No, I'm not! But I will be soon if you dumbos don't do something about it.

"I'm not sure," Luther mutters. "Her eyes looked like she was awake, like there was a spark, but she wasn't moving them."

That's because I can't! Urgh this is so frustrating.

My chest makes a strange, gurgling sound and suddenly, I can't breathe any longer.

I scream inside, wanting to gasp for air yet can't even open my mouth.

I'm dying and there's nothing I can do about it. No air.

My lungs are exploding, imploding, whatever, it hurts, but the darkness is closing in on me and there's no escape from it.

I fight, I lose, I get swallowed by unconsciousness.

# Twenty

Waking up is a bit of a shock. The world is more painful than I remember. I also don't remember my throat feeling so dry yet full.

I open my eyes and close them again when bright light shocks my brain into action. Ouch, that hurt.

"Em, can you hear me?"

His voice is far too loud. Shut up, Luther. Let me sleep.

I cough, trying to get whatever's blocking my throat out of there.

Oh. I can cough again. What a pleasant surprise.

I have dim memories bubble to the surface of my mind. Not being able to breathe. Hearing their voices. Sirens. People talking about me even though I could hear them. My men whispering sweet words that I couldn't respond to. It feels like it's been a long time since I first went into this strange state of being aware of the world but not being able to react to it.

Now, however, I can breathe and open my eyes.

Progress. Except that breathing isn't easy when there's something stuck in your throat.

I cough again, but it sounds more like I'm being strangled.

"I'll get a doctor," Ben says from afar. No, don't go. Stay here with me.

Of course, he doesn't do what I want, he never does.

None of them listen to my inner protests either when they use some kind of sucking thing, then remove the tube in my throat, then do the sucking thing again. When it's finally out and my throat has stopped itching, I look at them all, standing around my bed, looking a little uncomfortable.

"Hi," I say, sounding at least as croaky as I did back when I was last in hospital.

"Hi," all three of them reply as one.

While the doctors and nurses run checks on me - I'm a special case, apparently - the men fill the gaps in my memory.

"It was the letter," Alistair explains. "The paper had been soaked in a nerve agent that took a while to start working. If you hadn't run, you'd have died. Even so, you almost did."

Luther grimaces. "He'd staged it all. The word help scrawled on the wall was supposed to look like you had drawn it. He wanted us to suffer by seeing you dead, before then touching the letter ourselves and being exposed to the same poison. I don't know why he didn't stop you running away, maybe he was confident that nobody would be able to stop the poison from killing you."

His eyes have turned sad and I reach out, taking his hand. I'm physically weak, but inside, I feel strangely energetic, as if I've gained energy while being asleep.

"Luckily, this isn't the first time we've seen this," Ben continues the story. He looks tired. They've not told me yet how long I've been here, but I bet they were here with me most of the time.

"We dealt with a similar case about a year ago, so as soon as we had that suspicion, we cordoned off the house so nobody else could get exposed to the substance."

"Did you find him?" I ask hoarsely.

"Oh yes." There's a hardness in Luther's voice that I've not heard before. He's cold, deathly, without remorse. "He won't be troubling us ever again."

"Why?"

"Why did he do it?" Ben asks and I nod. "He was the brother of two of the men I shot. He wanted revenge. He must have been part of their team, so he knew our address and of your existence, but he waited until we'd let down our guard."

"You're not going to be alone ever again," Luther promises, but it almost sounds like a threat.

I squeeze his hand. "Yes, I will." He's about to protest when I squeeze his hand again to shut him up. I don't have the strength to argue. "I survived," I whisper. "I always survive."

Alistair chuckles. "That you do. I don't think I've ever met someone both as unlucky and as lucky as you."

I smile at that. "It's a special skill."

♥

We're not returning to Alistair's house. He's going to sell it; there are too many bad memories connected with it, and who knows who else might still be out there, wanting to hurt us in our home. For now, we're renting a large apartment in the centre of Edinburgh, but I know Alistair has been looking for a new house to buy. He's got more money than he can ever spend, so he's promised to find us the perfect house. Large, comfy, enough for all four of us. We all need our own space occasionally, and I have to admit that I miss having my own little studio flat. While the apartment is big, it still all belongs together and none of it is *mine*.

Today, I've sought some solitude in the office, which hasn't been used yet because the guys have been given three weeks' leave to look after me and find a new home for us. In a corner, the violin is waiting for me. I wanted to play yesterday, but was interrupted by one of the guys. This time, I close the door, hoping that it'll be enough of a deterrent. I'd love to lock it, but I know the guys wouldn't be able to deal with that yet. They're more traumatised by all that's happened than I am. For me, it was like being ill and then being healthy again. For them, it was their girlfriend almost dying.

I lift the violin and start playing without even thinking about what song to choose. It's a happy melody, something light and beautiful, yet it has some sad undertones that linger, penetrating my thoughts. Without stopping, I switch to another song, something that matches this new mood. Even though I'm playing it, it takes me a moment to recognise it. Albinoni. I've always loved that composer. I once played this song at school, accompanied by a teacher on the organ. I smile at the memory and close my eyes, giving myself to the music.

Time flows meaninglessly. The bow glides over the strings, producing sounds it shouldn't be able to. I've never fully managed to understand how such a small, wooden instrument can make such substantial music. How it can transcend the ordinary and become extraordinary.

I fully let go, pouring myself into the sound filling the room. I've not been this relaxed since I got back from the hospital.

Suddenly, there's a second melody meeting my own. Another violin. I open my eyes, almost expecting someone to stand in the room with me, but it's just me. I walk towards the door, still playing. There it is again. Now, I wish I hadn't closed the door as I can't open it while stroking my violin.

I change the melody a little, letting it fizzle out, turning it into a question. I still continue playing, but it's quiet now, just a wisp of a sound, waiting to be fanned back into being by the other violin.

And then it begins to sing. A duet with my violin, both of them embracing each other through their music. I don't know how I know what to play and how it perfectly matches what he is playing on the other side of the door, but by some strange kind of magic, it works.

We play like that for a long time. Minutes, hours, who knows. One song runs into another, without an ending, without a beginning. We just play, enjoying each other's company without seeing each other. The door stays shut, and if I wanted, I could probably interpret a lot into that, but my mind is filled with beautiful music that dispels any deep thoughts.

When we finish, we do it together. The final vibrato shows me how tired my muscles are and I let my arms lower, exhausted. I stand there, holding the violin and the bow, not moving, not knowing what to do. Will I break the spell by opening the door?

My hands are shaking slightly, so I put the violin back into the corner, almost whispering a thank you, but then realising how crazy that would be.

The door clicks open behind me and I turn, falling right into Alistair's arms. His mouth seeks mine, just like his music did moments ago, and we kiss, merging even more than we already did. Instead of playing with our violins, we now play an intricate dance of tongues and lips. His taste is all I want to taste, his heartbeat all I want to feel against my chest.

I wrap my arms around his back, holding him as tight as I can. A strange feeling has entered my heart, the fear of losing him. Not that I'm ever going to let that happen. He's mine, and this strange, magical duet has just proven that once again.

His lips move from my mouth over my cheek up to my ear. He gently bites my earlobe, then whispers the words I've been waiting for. I smile and nudge him to the chair in front of the desk, where we can be more comfortable. Our duet isn't over yet.

"I need more onions!" Ben shouts over the noise and Alistair throws him some. Ben catches them effortlessly and starts chopping them, adding the pieces to the giant bowl in front of him. I smile and continue stirring the broth like Luther instructed me to. The soup kitchen didn't know what hit them when Luther appeared with suggestions about what to cook. They basically told him that he had free reign as long as nobody complained. So far, nobody has. They all love his cooking, which doesn't surprise me in the slightest. He's amazing at this.

"Are we out of carrots?" Alistair asks, searching the plastic boxes underneath the counter.

"There should be more in the storage chamber," I tell him, not taking my eyes off the broth. Last week, I managed to burn the eggs I was supposed to watch, so this time I'm not going to look away. I'm terrible at cooking, but here, I'm not doing it for myself. I'm doing it for the dozens of people waiting outside in the community hall.

We're volunteering at the soup kitchen once a week. Sometimes, I see familiar faces, people I met when I was living on the streets, but we rarely talk. I didn't speak to them when I was still sleeping rough, and I doubt any of them recognise me. For them, we're just some people who want to do something good, some rich folks with money to spare. That we are, but they don't know how we're making it. They don't know how Luther has a slowly healing gash on his thigh after he was attacked on a recent mission. They don't know that our house is like a fortress full of security systems and traps for potential intruders. They don't know that I used to be one of them.

My world has changed so much. From the abused girlfriend to a SOCA employee, helping solve crimes and fight injustice. It sounds a bit like a dream and sometimes, I actually pinch myself just to make sure it's real.

One week ago, I finally got my cast removed. My foot still looks pale and strange, as if it doesn't quite belong to my body, but I can deal with that. I'm having physiotherapy twice a week, and I've started joining the guys downstairs in the gym. Alistair is teaching me self-defence and has promised we're going to do some offensive moves as well. I never want to be helpless again.

"There are no carrots," Alistair reports, returning from checking the storage.

"Seriously?" Luther asks, annoyance tainting his voice. "But I need them. Otherwise the potatoes will overshadow the taste of carrots and parsnips."

"Lou, nobody will notice," I reassure him. "As long as

it's warm and tastes good, I don't think anyone cares about the potato-carrot-ratio."

He looks disgruntled, but takes the bowl of diced onions Ben hands him and begins to fry them.

"Can't you go and buy some carrots?" he mutters, the question probably directed at Alistair.

"No, I'm busy with peeling parsnips, or do you want me to stop doing that?"

"Boys, it will all be okay," I chuckle. "It will be delicious. Luther, does the broth need more salt?"

It's fun how easy he is to distract. He takes a spoon and tastes the broth.

"Perfect," he says with a grin, then looks me straight in the eyes. "Just like you."

I hit him with the wooden spoon I'm wielding. "You need to work on your pick up lines."

He laughs and rubs his arm. "I don't think I will need any of those for you. I've already picked you."

A warm feeling spreads through my stomach. "No, you haven't. It was *me* who picked you."

A knock on the door stops our banter.

It's Mrs Darlington, the organiser of the soup kitchen.

"There's someone from the newspaper out there. She's heard rumours and would like to interview you."

I look at her, confused. "Rumours about what?"

"Someone who used to be homeless now working here. She wants to see if it's a success story of leaving the streets and becoming a part of society again."

I grimace.

"Believe me, I was a part of society before. Society

isn't just people living in their houses, going to work every day, having families. Society is all of us, no matter if we're rich or poor, unlucky or successful. Instead of interviewing me, she should interview someone out there, one of the people waiting for food. They're far more interesting. I got help, they haven't yet. Maybe she can get involved in helping them."

Mrs Darlington stares at me, then smiles. "I'll pass it on. It smells delicious, by the way."

Once she's gone, Luther slips an arm around my waist.

"Well said."

I shrug. "It's not like I can appear in the paper with my new job. We have to stay below the radar, right?"

He nods. "Yes, we do. I guess you could do the interview, if you really wanted, and just not let them include a photograph, but it's always better to stay hidden. We work from the shadows."

Ben laughs from behind me. "Although we're the light that dispels the shadows."

"Smooth." Luther throws a towel at his friend. "Let's get this soup done, even without enough carrots. We have a crowd to feed."

♥

The long benches are cold and not particularly comfy, but the warm soup in my belly makes up for it. Now that everyone has left, we're alone in the community hall, enjoying the leftovers. Two volunteers have started doing the dishes and we should probably join them soon, but right now, we're all sitting together in comfortable silence.

I wonder what the guys are thinking about. The food? The people we fed? The cold waiting for them outside?

I've been thinking about that a lot. I've donated most of the compensation money I got to Social Bite, a local organisation helping people off the streets and back into employment. I've kept some back that will help me be independent and I used some of it to pay off my debts, both my student debts and the money Alistair spent on my clothes and the phone. We had a bit of a fight about it, but eventually he accepted that it was important for me to pay him. In return, I've allowed him to give me occasional presents, but nothing that I need to live. I pay for that myself. I *need* to be independent, even though I live with them and share their lives.

For now, I don't need to worry about money again. I work full time for SOCA, they pay well, and as our house belongs to Alistair, I live there rent free. We've found the most beautiful villa on the outskirts of the city with view of the hills. There's a ski slope not far from us that Ben is going to take me to once my leg is fully healed. It takes a while to get into town but I do a lot of my translations from home. While I've met some of the guys' colleagues in their office, I much prefer working on my laptop in the living room, sometimes together with Alistair, who also prefers to stay home. The other two do a lot of field work, as they always have. None of us is made for a typical nine to five office job.

"Penny for your thoughts?" Ben asks, a hint of his inquisitive persona sparkling behind his eyes.

I shrug. "Just thinking that I'm happy. And lucky. Penny for yours?"

He doesn't reply immediately and his expression darkens. "My sister. I wish she'd found a way out like you did."

I reach out and squeeze his right hand. He's balled the other into a fist.

"There was nothing you could do," I say gently. "But you helped me. You helped so many others. Did you see how grateful everyone was today? All we did was make food but that simple gesture left an impression on them. Most of the people you help in your job will never even know that you prevented them from coming to harm. You're an amazing person, Ben, don't you ever doubt that."

He doesn't reply, but he turns until his eyes lock with mine. There's pain in them, so much pain, but I know he's not as broken as he might feel just now. He didn't just help me to get me off the streets. He also did it to help himself, even though he did it unknowingly.

Same with Alistair. We visited his mother last week. She doesn't remember him, she has no idea he's her son, but we still spend some time with her. She thought we were just a nice couple, strangers who sat with her in a cafe, who gave her some company. She won't remember by now that we ever met. Alistair said that in the beginning, he tried to make her remember; that he visited her every day, but it became painful for both of them. Now he stays away, mostly, and she's happier that way according to her doctors. I'm glad we went though. It made me understand him a little more.

Ben kisses me, distracting me from my thoughts once again. I smile and return his kiss. He tastes like salt and soup and it's probably the same for me.

When we break apart, Luther clears his throat.

"We have a surprise for you."

Even that sentence surprises me. Why would they have something for me? It's three months until my birthday and two weeks until Christmas.

"It wasn't planned," Alistair whispers. "Luther clicked the wrong button."

Luther clears his throat again. "Let's go outside. It's in the car."

We leave our empty bowls on the table and head out into the cold. There's a van parked behind our car. Luther takes a key from his pocket and hands it to me, nodding towards the van's back door.

He doesn't respond to my questioning look, so I go and unlock the door. The van is full of cardboard boxes.

I turn around. "What's this about?"

Alistair is trying very hard not to laugh. "Open one of them."

I do as he asks, using the van key to cut through the tape. Inside is...

I laugh, and laugh, and laugh even more. Then I turn and hug Luther, still giggling like a madwoman.

"I was wondering why it was so expensive," he says with a chuckle. "I thought it was grams when it was actually kilograms."

I step back and look at him, laughter still bubbling up my throat.

"You." I emphasise every word. "Bought. Me. A. Van. Full. Of. Cocoa."

He grins widely. "Shall I make you a hot chocolate?"

My eyes are teary from all the laughing. I blink up at him and nod.

"That would be lovely."

Alistair picks me up and carries me inside, while Luther is talking about a chocolate recipe book he saw and Ben is trying to contain his laughter.

We're a crazy bunch, and I'm absolutely loving it.

*Want more of Em and her men? Continue their story in* **Loving Heart**, *a sequel involving Valentine's Day and a Royal mission.*

*If you enjoyed this book, you might also like* **Broken Spirit**, *a reverse harem also featuring Mrs M and SOCA, but a lot darker than this one.*

*For all the latest releases, author updates and cat pictures, subscribe to my newsletter:* **skyemackinnon.com/ newsletter**

*Read on for a sample, as well as for two recipes!*

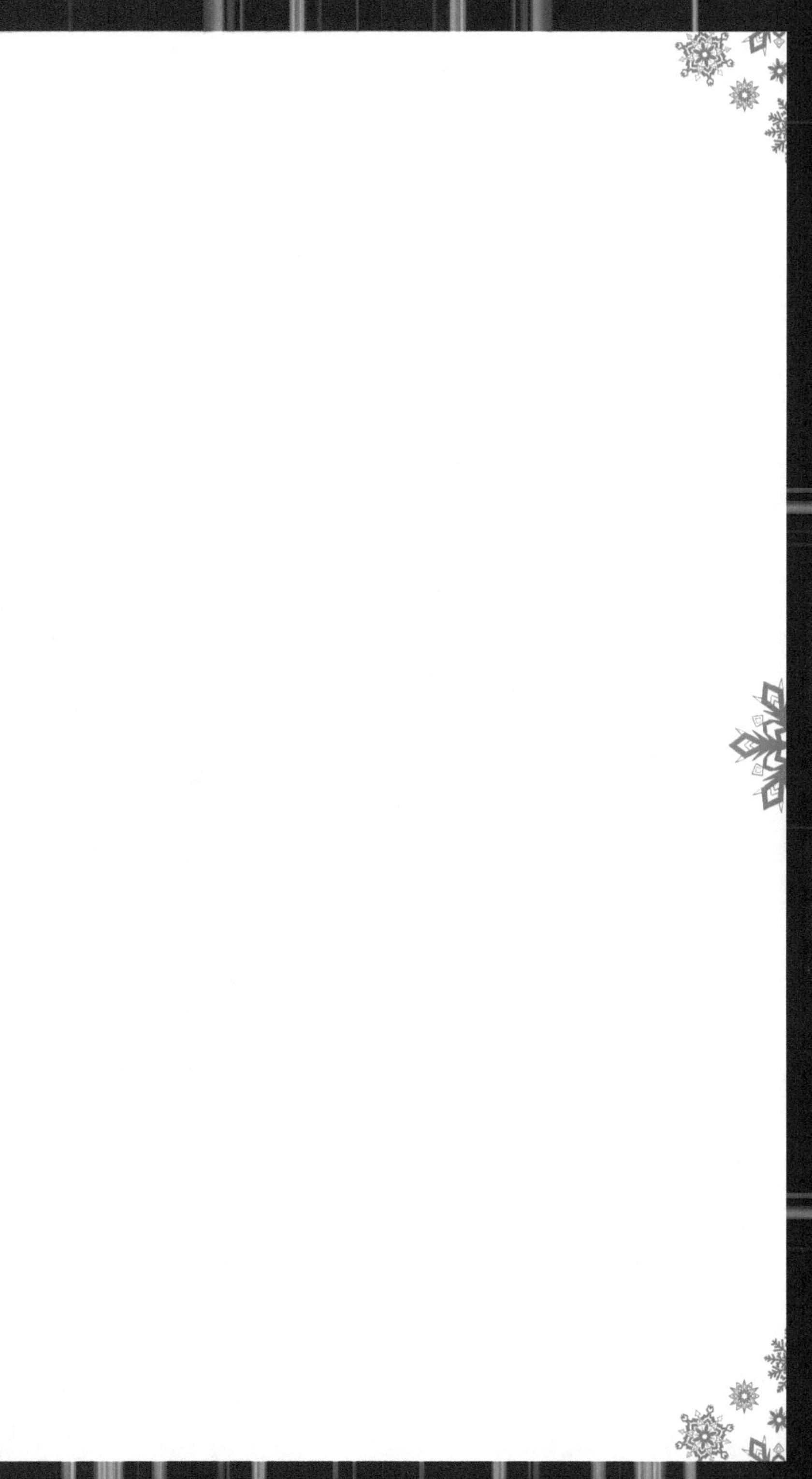

**Dear readers,**

I hope you're in the mood for some hot chocolate now! Read on for a recipe!

If you're also in the mood to join the fight against homelessness, there's a list of organisations you can support on theBig Issue UK website.

In Scotland,Social Bite is on a mission to end homelessness and they've had some great success with some of their initiatives. Their work is so inspiring that one winter, I spent a night outside to raise money for them, and I've also donated some of my royalties to their cause.

We all can do something - even if it's as simple as buying someone a hot chocolate...

# Luther's Chocolate Mug Cake Recipe

## INGREDIENTS

- 4 tbsp self-raising flour
- 4 tbsp caster sugar
- 2 tbsp cocoa powder
- 1 medium egg
- 3 tbsp milk
- 3 tbsp vegetable oil or sunflower oil
- a few drops of vanilla essence or other essence
- 2 tbsp chocolate chips (optional)

## HOW TO DO IT

1. Add the flour, sugar and cocoa powder to the
   largest mug you have and mix. Add the egg
   and mix, then add the other liquid
   ingredients. Mix until smooth, before adding

the chocolate chips and mixing again. Em prefers dark chocolate chips.

2. Centre your mug in the middle of the microwave and cook on high for 1½ -2 mins, or until it has stopped rising and is firm to the touch. Don't forget to watch it rise as it cooks!

3. Eat! You can add ice cream or whipped cream to make it even more calorific.

# Mrs M's Hot Chocolate Recipe

## INGREDIENTS

- 2 tablespoons unsweetened cocoa powder
- 1 to 2 tablespoons sugar (depending on how sweet you like it)
- Pinch of salt
- 1 cup milk or any combination of milk, half-and-half, or cream
- 1/4 teaspoon vanilla extract

## HOW TO DO IT

Whisk together the cocoa, sugar, salt, and about 2 tablespoons milk in a small saucepan over medium-low heat until both the cocoa and sugar are dissolved. Whisk in the rest of the milk and heat it over medium heat, whisking occasionally, until it is hot. Stir in the vanilla and serve. Emily likes it with cream and chocolate sprinkles.

# Blurb: Broken Spirit

**Did they come to save or break her heart?**

Laya is called the Princess, but in fact, she's nothing but a slave to her husband and cult leader Andros. Abused and suppressed, she has no hope of escape until three new recruits enter her life.

They quickly take to living in the compound, but Laya can't help feeling that they're different. That they might not believe in what they have to do for Andros. That they aren't as cold and cruel as him.

With Andros planning his cruellest deed yet, she needs to escape - but will these three men be her salvation or her doom?

****Trigger warning: This is a dark story that contains violence, sexual abuse, mentions of suicide and death. Read at your own discretion.****

# Sample: Broken Spirit

The sound of the whip being unfurled is worse than the pain to come. The tingling of anticipation is running over my skin, preparing my nerve endings for the beating that he's about to unleash on my naked body.

*Pain is salvation.*

I steel my mind like he taught me.

*Discipline leads to redemption.*

He only wants to help. That's why he's going to whip me.

*Suffering brings peace.*

Without pain, I won't be able to be freed of this mortal world. I won't be able to ascend with the Prophet and the others. The pain is necessary.

I take a deep breath, readying myself.

"Begin."

♥

His ugly scent still hangs in the air even after he's long gone. It's all over my skin, reminding me of what just happened. I want to cry and have a shower, but the first won't do any good and the second is forbidden. It's still two more days until I'm allowed my next shower.

I pull my blanket closer, but then throw it away when its touch reminds me of the marks he's left on me. It's too rough, just like his hands. I breathe in deep through my mouth, but can't stop a bit of his scent getting trapped in my nose. His breath always reminds me of something rotten, something so dead inside that it's almost impossible to hide. But he hides it well. To the others, he's a holy man, a Prophet. To me, he's the devil.

At least he'll be busy until later today. Time for me to prepare for his next beating. It's one of those days when he's angry and needs someone to let out his frustrations on. He told me once that with every mark on my skin, his anger gets less. It's a sign for him that he's working on it.

That's what he sees it as. Dealing with his problems. I'm the canvas to paint his anger onto.

A few more hours until he's back. It's harder knowing what's to come than when it's one of his impulsive attacks. Those I can usually avoid by staying in the company of the other women. He doesn't do it in front of people. He's their leader, he needs to show how he's the perfect person. The chosen one. The Prophet. The King.

Inside though, he's rotten to the core. Nothing royal in there. Just hate and violence and anger and pride. All the sins he preaches against are somewhere in him. Maybe that's why he's so passionate about eradicating them. If everybody else is without sin, maybe he will be, too.

I wish he'd allow us some cream to put on the bruises, but that's forbidden. When I first moved here, I thought it was a good thing that cosmetics are banned in the compound. Now, I see it differently. If he puts bruises on me, he should give me something to treat them.

He always makes sure that the bruises stay below the neckline. I'm not allowed to wear revealing shirts anyway, none of us are. Our simple uniform includes a long-sleeved blouse and a skirt that reaches our ankles. Together with our shorn heads, we're hard to tell apart. That's how it's supposed to be. We're all one family, one community, where nobody is better than the others. Except for Andros, of course.

Twenty women, all thin as sticks, heads bowed, quiet and demure. But still, I'm different, even though I don't want to be. I'm wearing a golden circlet on my shaved head, telling everyone that I'm the Prophet's wife. His Princess. He's the King, but he is so far above us all that it would be silly to call me his queen. No, I'm the Princess, and that keeps me apart from the other women in the compound.

Only at dawn and dusk, when we recite the words of our community, we're all the same. When the fog hangs deep in the valley, we assemble in the clearing in the centre of the village and chant together:

*Discipline leads to redemption.*
*Suffering brings peace.*
*Obedience inspires happiness.*
*Pain is salvation.*

*The Angel is our shield and our refuge.*

It's the mantra I hear every day. I say it every day. And once, I believed it. Maybe I still do.

Back then, I said those words with fervour and passion. But that all changed long ago and now, it's empty words for me. I say them because it's expected of me. Because I will be punished if I don't. As the Princess, I need to be an example, both in good deeds and in my punishments. My husband likes to show everyone how women should be treated. The bruises stay beneath my clothes, but there are other ways to punish and humiliate. Andros knows every single one of them.

I once admired him for his intelligence and creativity. Now I fear him for coming up with yet another method of punishment. But then I remember that I deserve it, and it hurts less.

We all deserve to suffer.

*Suffering brings peace.*

Does something become true if you say it often enough? Does the universe listen and make it so?

If so, then I will be at peace. I have suffered a lot. Not just me, we all have. Suffering is at the core of our community. We built it up from scratch, we fought with the inhospitable land to survive. There are no modern conveniences out here; we are on our own. Suffering has been with us from day one.

How long has it been since then? Five years? Six? Time has lost its meaning.

Some days, I'm still happy I live here, away from society, together with men and women sworn to a simpler life. Other days, all I want to do is run.

Pain flares up around my right ankle and I bite back a groan. It always does that when I think of leaving. The thin silver bracelet he once put on me has merged with my flesh, burned into my skin. It was the first and only time I ever tried to run away.

He said that if I ever tried it again, he'd use the same blowtorch on my head until the golden circlet I'm forced to wear melts and permanently becomes part of me.

I put a hand on my ankle, the coolness of my skin a soothing relief for the pain that isn't really there. It's just a memory. The pain everywhere else is very real, though. Why am I focussing on my ankle when my stomach feels like a car has run me over?

It's probably some kind of self-preservation mechanism.

I roll to my other side to take the pressure off my bruised ribs. Spots dance along my vision as the pounding in my head starts anew.

How did a life without pain feel like? Was I happier back then?

We're taught to forget the past, to focus on the present and on our future. Especially on our future. Everything we do is to make sure that we'll transcend once we leave this life behind. Andros says that so far, he is the only one who's ready to ascend, but he's staying behind to make sure that we reach the same level of preparation. He's generous like that, sharing his wisdom and knowledge. Other Prophets may have just left, preferring to be with the Angel.

Not Andros, though. He cares for all of us, his flock,

even though his methods can be rough. At least I think that's what he believes.

I'm not quite sure if I believe it. I've not known what's real and what isn't for a long time. I hope that Paradise is real. That way, all what we're going through is going to be worth it.

*Discipline leads to redemption.*

Our daily struggles, the punishments, the harsh rules, it's all to prepare us for ascension. Right now, we're not worthy of the Angel's attention. But soon, we will be. Andros will make sure of it.

I focus on that thought. No matter how much I despise Andros, he is the Prophet. The pain will only be temporary.

But it's so hard to believe. Everything hurts, even lying on the hard wooden floor is painful. I think he may have cracked my ribs again. Every breath is an ache in my chest, but I'm not ready to stop breathing yet. I'm not ready.

A gentle knock on the door has me sit up.

Petal enters, searching the room for me before her eyes spot me in the corner.

"How bad is it?" she asks quietly and hurries to me.

"It's been worse," I reply with a grimace and take the glass of water she's offering me.

"Pain is salvation," Petal says, her expression full of hope and conviction. She may be kind to me, but she's also one of Andros's most passionate followers. She was one of the first, and likely she'll be the first of his flock to ascend, too.

She takes back the glass and hands me a wet cloth.

We're not allowed to put salve on our wounds, but at least the coolness of the water will provide some relief. I start patting my forehead to remove the sweat and the tears. If Andros sees me like this, weak and frail, it will only make him angry.

While I begin to gently rub away the blood on my shoulders, Petal takes another cloth and cleans my back. Every single touch hurts, but it's a better pain than that of the whip, because it's not intentional.

"He'll be late," the older woman informs me. "There are three new applicants and he's decided to interview them right away. Three men, I think, but I only got a quick look before he told me to look after you."

He didn't send her because he's kind. No, he wants a clean canvas for later to continue his painting. The existing stripes of wounds and barely healed scars don't bother him, but dried blood does. It looks dirty, he says, so he always sends one of the other women to make me clean again.

"Where are they from?" I ask her, but she clucks her tongue in disapproval. Their past doesn't matter. We shouldn't question where they come from, just where they're going.

"If he agrees to take them in as novices, we'll have an assembly tonight," she informs me instead of answering my question.

I suppress a sigh. If there's an assembly, I have to leave our hut, which means wearing my scratchy, heavy robe on my open wounds. It's going to be even more painful than it is now.

The last time we had new people join our community

is months ago. Maybe even a year. Now that we're completely self-sufficient, we don't communicate with the outside world any longer. Andros is the only one who leaves occasionally to buy supplies. Nobody knows we exist. Sometimes, Andros talks about wanting to spread the message of the Angel so that more people can be saved, but then he decides that we're enough followers. If we'd accept new people, it would take them long to adjust and to learn. Our own ascension would be delayed, and Andros wouldn't like that. He's stayed here with us for too long already. He wants to ascend and join the Angel, just like we all do.

"Let's pray," Petal says, and sits down by my side, her hands on her knees, turned upward so that the blessings of the Angel can flow into her. I take the same position, trying not to wince as pain flows through me. This beating was worse than the ones before, and I know it's going to take a while to heal.

"Angel, your words are salvation," Petal begins and I join her, my mind focussing on the mantras and forgetting the pain.

❤

*Continue reading* Broken Spirit, *available in my shop, at retailers and in libraries.*

# Buy your books direct from the author

GET 20% OFF YOUR NEXT EBOOK OR AUDIOBOOK!

USE CODE BOOKWORMS AT SKYEMACKINNON.COM/SHOP

EBOOKS, AUDIOBOOKS, PRINT BOOKS, MERCHANDISE & MORE

# About the Author

Skye MacKinnon is a Scottish romance author who was raised by elves in the mystical Highlands and calls the Loch Ness monster her friend. Her bestselling books weave together romance with action, suspense and whimsical humour, creating page-turners filled with strong heroines, alpha heroes and loveable monsters.

Whether she's writing about aliens in kilts, hunky Vikings or cat shifter assassins, Skye likes to put a new spin on familiar tropes. Some of her heroines don't have to choose, some fall in love with other women, and others get abducted by clueless aliens.

Skye lives with her bossy cat on the west coast of Scotland and uses the dramatic views from her office as an inspiration, no matter whether she writes fantasy, paranormal or science fiction romance. Until she gets abducted by aliens, that is.

Subscribe to her newsletter:
**skyemackinnon.com/newsletter**

# Also by Skye MacKinnon

Find all of Skye's books on her website, **skyemackinnon.com**, where you can also order signed paperbacks and swag. Many of her books are available as audiobooks.

## PARANORMAL & FANTASY ROMANCE

- **Claiming Her Bears** (post-apocalyptic shifter reverse harem)
- **Daughter of Winter** (fantasy reverse harem)
- **Catnip Assassins** (urban fantasy reverse harem)
- **Infernal Descent** (paranormal reverse harem based on Dante's Inferno, co-written with Bea Paige)
- **Seven Wardens** (fantasy reverse harem co-written with Laura Greenwood)
- **The Lost Siren** (post-apocalyptic, paranormal reverse harem co-written with Liza Street)

# SCIENCE FICTION ROMANCE

- **Starlight Highlanders Mail Order Brides** (sci-fi m/f romance, part of the Intergalactic Dating Agency)
- **Starlight Vikings** (sci-fi m/f romance, part of the Intergalactic Dating Agency)
- **Starlight Mermen** (sci-fi m/f romance, part of the Intergalactic Dating Agency)
- **Starlight Monsters** (m/f romance)
- **The Intergalactic Guide to Humans** (sci-fi romance with various pairings)
- **Between Rebels** (sci-fi reverse harem set in the Planet Athion shared world)
- **The Mars Diaries** (sci-fi reverse harem)
- **Through the Gates** (dystopian reverse harem co-written with Rebecca Royce)
- **Aliens and Animals** (f/f sci-fi romance co-written with Arizona Tape)

# OTHER SERIES

- **Academy of Time** (time travel academy standalones, reverse harem and m/f)
- **Defiance** (contemporary reverse harem with a hint of thriller/suspense)

# STANDALONES

- Song of Souls – m/f fantasy romance, fairy tale retelling
- Wings of Time and Fate - YA fantasy
- Highland Butterflies – lesbian romance

# BOX SETS

- Daggers & Destiny – a Skye MacKinnon starter
library
- Stars & Seduction - a Sci-Fi Romance starter
library